WE WERE

NEVER

MEANT TO BE

WE WERE
NEVER
MEANT TO BE

LOVING YOU WAS NOT ENOUGH

Palle Vasu

AMARYLLIS

AMARYLLIS

An imprint of Manjul Publishing House Pvt. Ltd.
• C-16, Sector 3, Noida, Uttar Pradesh 201 301, India
Website: www.manjulindia.com

Registered Office:
• 2nd Floor, Usha Preet Complex, 42 Malviya Nagar,
Bhopal 462 003 – India

Distribution Centres
Ahmedabad, Bengaluru, Chennai, Hyderabad,
Kochi, Kolkata, Mumbai, Noida, Pune

We Were Never Meant to Be: Loving You Was Not Enough by Palle Vasu

This edition published in paperback by
Amaryllis, an imprint of Manjul Publishing House in 2025

ISBN 978-93-5543-381-7

Printed and bound in India by Repro India Limited

*This book is dedicated to everyone who carries the weight of
unrequited love and struggles mentally in pursuit
of an illusion.
I hope you find peace in your journey.*

Contents

Thank you, Krishna

I want to thank Lord Krishna, who has always stood by His devotees, including me. During my days of struggle, in every moment, I have tried to worship Him. He will find mention in all the books I write.

He is everything.

Preface

～

Love stories often speak of togetherness, of two hearts finding their way to each other. But what about the love that never had a destination, but was only a journey? *We Were Never Meant to Be* is a story of such love—one that existed in silence, thrived in longing, and remained despite knowing it was never meant to be.

This book is not about heartbreak; it is about love in its rawest form—the kind that asks for nothing in return, yet never fades. It is about cherishing moments that never turned into memories, about holding on without expecting to be held back.

Through these pages, you will find emotions that speak louder than words, feelings that linger beyond time, and a love story that was never written in fate but was lived nonetheless.

For those who have ever loved without expectation, for those who have felt deeply in silence—this book is for you.

—Palle Vasu

ONE

MATHURA

~

The sounds of the *antyeshti* and the crowd's cries rang in my ears. I couldn't budge an inch. My body seemed like lead, my chest constricted, as if everything weighed on me all at once. My eyes lost focus, and for a second, the floor felt like it was giving way. A knot grew in my throat, but I couldn't speak. I was falling apart—bit by bit, with agonising slowness.

A Forest Range Officer (FRO) ran towards me from the meeting room, shouting, 'Hey, Vasu! How many times do I have to tell you to serve tea after the snacks?'

I was still paralysed by the echoes of the antyeshti.

The FRO grabbed my shoulder and shook me. 'Bring the tea fast! Everyone's waiting in the meeting room. DFO sir has already asked for it twice!'

His voice snapped me back to reality. He turned and rushed back into the meeting room which was surrounded by lush foliage from the nursery plantation. The office

1

building was right behind it. I grabbed the tea flask, tray, and cups from a cotton box, setting them up on a table. I filled each cup with tea, placed them on the tray, and walked to the meeting room.

The oval meeting table inside was crammed with attendees, and people were sitting behind them, with hardly breathing space. My task was simple but challenging: to serve tea to everyone in that crowded room.

Holding the tray tightly, I carefully walked around the room, placing cups on desks one by one. At times, the tray wobbled, threatening to spill, but I managed to hold steady. Finally, I reached the last seat.

A man in his mid-thirties sitting nearby gestured for me to come closer. Curious, I bent down as he whispered, 'You're Vasu, right?'

'What?' I asked softly, trying not to disturb the presentation on wildlife crimes.

'Are you Mr Vasu?' he asked again.

'Yes, sir. I'm Vasu, O.S.,' I replied—clearly this time. 'Author of *Forest Sentinel*, right?'

'Yes, sir.'

He extended his hand with a smile. 'Your book is incredible. The humour and storytelling are top-notch. It's one of the best I've ever read.'

I shook his hand and thanked him, walking out of the room with quiet pride. For an artist, an author, or even a singer, it's not about the money that they earn. It is about true happiness they feel when someone acknowledges and appreciates their work. It feels like taking a long, peaceful nap after ten days of sleepless nights.

The meeting eventually ended, and people began filing out of the room, including my boss, the DFO. I hurried inside to collect the used cups and stacked them neatly near the washbasin. After some time, I climbed the stairs to the dining area, where my boss was waiting for his meal.

The forest complex was simple, with a few buildings: the meeting room, offices for the DFO, FDO and FRO, and a couple of abandoned structures. The DFO's office was a two-storey building, with small guest suites with dining and kitchen on the top floor.

After lunch, the DFO called his driver, climbed into his Toyota Crysta, and headed into the forest to inspect a beat. I sat at a computer in the office and started writing my book *The Revoken Naxalism*.

My phone rang—it was an anonymous number. 'Hello?' I answered. 'Who's this?'

'I'm Sriram, the FRO.'

'Good evening, sir,' I greeted him. 'Why did you kill three people?'

I froze. Last night, I had a dream that I assassinated three people. My heart left my body—I was unable to move. It wasn't a dream. It was real.

'Hello?'

I came back to my senses. 'Sir! Sir! I'm not the one!' 'What? You're not the author?'

'Yes, sir, but I've never seen blood!'

'Mean it,' he said.

'Sir, am I the culprit of three murders?' 'Of course, you are!'

'Sir, I thought it was a dream!'

'But you killed three people in quite the gruesome manner!'

'Sir, am I going to be arrested now?' My legs started shaking. My whole body trembled, breaking out in sweat. Srikanth and Srilatha, my colleagues, rushed towards me. 'What happened?' they asked while I was still speaking on the phone.

I wiped my sweat and asked again, 'Sir, am I going to jail now?'

'Of course! You deserve that!' 'Jail?!' Srikanth shouted.

'Sir, I don't remember anything! How could I kill a person—let alone three—so brutally?'

'That's what I'm asking. Why did you kill three innocent people?'

The news spread across the office. Everyone gathered around. Some whispered, 'I know an MLA,' 'I know an IPS officer,' but I was in shock.

'You have to be in jail, Vasu,' the FRO said after a pause.

'Yes, sir. I don't deserve to live. I never thought I could kill someone.'

'Then who will write another book, you idiot? You have to stay alive!'

MATHURA

'What?' I paused for a minute. 'Sir, whom did I kill?' I put the call on the loudspeaker.

'Erraiah, Sravan, Arjun.'

Everyone around me started laughing.

I felt instant relief. Those were the characters from my book!

He spoke again. 'What happened? Why is everyone laughing? Is this funny? Do you know how well-written those characters were?'

'Sir, it's just a book! Why are you so deeply involved in it?'

'Just a book? How could you say that, Vasu? You are its author!'

Finally I understood his disappointment. But how could a person be so attached to a book—especially mine? This wasn't the first time people expressed their emotions like this. It had happened many times before—people got really attached to my characters.

'It's okay, Vasu. This is the best book I've ever read. Actually, it's my first book, but perhaps the best. The humour and thrill you introduced in the story—I have no words to express. It's just fantastic!'

'Really? Thank you, sir!' I said and cut the call.

Everyone returned to their tables, looking at their computer screens, some busy with office calls, just like before.

The Following Day

'Have you taken the keys?' The sun was shining so brightly. Here, take this umbrella,' mom said.

'Mom, it's okay.' I packed my luggage, zipped it, and lifted the bag.

My mom swiftly went to the garden and returned with something . I slowly stepped out of the house and stood at the entrance.

'Here you go, keep it in your pocket,' she said, handing me a tulsi leaf.

Holding the leaf, I asked my mother, 'Why, mom? Why this?' I wanted to argue, but I felt it would take too much time.

'Tulsi is good for travelling,' she began, launching into an explanation. I immediately started walking to save time. 'Bye! Travel safe! Buy a water bottle! Eat on time!' my mother yelled after me, but I wasn't really listening to her words.

I reached the bus stop to catch a bus to Chandrapur, Maharashtra, where I would stay with my sister for a few days.

There was utter silence at the bus stop. A few dogs were playing, and some monkeys could be seen sitting on the wall surrounding of the bus stop. Everything looked peaceful. They weren't like corporate slaves, rushing to their offices by 6 a.m.

MATHURA

I sat on the table at the bus stand, my legs swinging slightly as I vibed to Emiway's *Not Afraid*. The beats echoed in my ears, and for a moment, everything around me faded. It was just me, the music, and my thoughts—until, suddenly, something shifted.

I felt myself sinking deeper into consciousness, completely lost in the song. It wasn't just music anymore; it was a trance, pulling me in, making me question everything, yet giving me a strange sense of peace.

After a while, I reached my sister's home and placed my bag in the living room. The familiar warmth of home surrounded me, but my mind was still wandering.

It was Raksha Bandhan. The scent of freshly made sweets filled the air as my sister busied herself in the kitchen. My brother-in-law was on his way back from the office. It was a moment of celebration, a day meant for bonding and happiness. But as much as I wanted to feel present, boredom crept in.

I grabbed my diary, flipping through its pages. I wanted to write, to let my thoughts spill onto paper, but I was stuck. My mind was a mess. I didn't know where to start or what to write about.

Just then, my sister's phone rang from the bedroom, its sound blending with the hissing of the cooker. She didn't not hear the ringtone. I walked to the bedroom to pick it up. The screen flashed my brother-in-law's name.

I answered, pressing the phone to my ear.

But before I could say anything, a sudden, deafening lorry horn blasted through the speaker, making me flinch. I immediately pulled the phone away, my heart racing.

Then, a voice spoke. 'Hello?'

It wasn't my brother-in-law.

'Hello? Hello? Are you there?' The voice was urgent, struggling to cut through the heavy traffic noise in the background.

'The person carrying this phone has met with an accident. Please reach Gandhi Chowk immediately.'

The call ended.

For a second I froze even as I could hear the fan whirring, the cooker whistling, life going on around me.

My sister walked in, holding a fresh, half-made sweet in a spoon. She smiled.

'Hey Vikram, taste this!' She held it up to my face. I didn't respond.

She frowned. 'What happened? Why do you look so dejected suddenly?'

I took a deep breath, forcing the words out. 'Akka... Bava met with an accident. He's at Gandhi Chowk.'

Her face went pale. 'What?!' she gasped.

'Don't worry, Akka. He's fine. I'll take him to the hospital. You stay here and handle things,' I reassured her, even though, deep down, I had no idea if he was truly fine. I rushed out, my heart pounding with every step. The streets blurred past as I rode towards Gandhi Chowk, my mind filled with worst-case scenarios. But when I arrived, I saw he was injured but conscious. A wave of relief washed over me.

He wasn't in a critical condition, but I didn't want to take any risks. I took him to the nearest multi-speciality hospital.

The staff quickly attended to him, bandaging his head and hands. He would be fine, they said.

After meeting the doctor, we were heading back, and as usual, I plugged in my earphones, letting Eminem's voice fill my mind, trying to drown out the stress of the evening. Then, out of nowhere—BAM! A girl dashed into me.

For a moment, everything stopped.

She was stunning—not just in a way that made you look, but in a way that made you pause and truly see.

Her long, dark hair cascaded over her shoulders, catching the dim streetlights like waves reflecting the setting sun. Her deep brown eyes held something I couldn't quite place—something intense, something unspoken. Her skin had the warmth of monsoon-kissed earth, glowing under the night sky. A small bindi rested between her brows, adding to her effortless elegance.

She looked at me, startled. 'Sorry,' she mumbled quickly, then walked away.

But something caught my eye—a diary on the ground where she had bumped into me.

She didn't notice. She didn't even turn. Within seconds, she had disappeared into the crowd.

I picked up the diary and took it home.

My sister still looked a little worried about my Bava. She had always told him to take the car to the office, but he insisted on riding his bike. Maybe today was a lesson. Later in the evening, she tied the rakhi on my wrist—a small, quiet moment between us—a moment of tradition, of love.

After that, I slumped onto the sofa, flipping open the diary I had found.

Just then—knock, knock. Someone was at the door.

I opened it. And there she was—the girl from the hospital.

For a moment, we just stared at each other. Then, I realised I had her diary.

I quickly handed it to her.

I was following you ever since I saw my diary in your hands outside the hospital. I panicked, but thank God I found it. She turned to leave. Without thinking, I followed her to the road.

'Your name?' I asked.

She stopped and turned slightly. 'Mathura,' she replied, eyeing me cautiously. 'And you?'

'Vasu. What do you do? Are you a writer?' 'Nope, I'm a surgeon. You?'

'I'm a writer.'

She tilted her head slightly. 'Writer?' She sounded doubtful.

I nodded. 'I write books,' I said, pulling out my phone to show her *Forest Sentinel*. Maybe, just maybe, I could make a sale.

She glanced at it. 'Nice,' she said, then got into an auto. 'Can I come with you? I'll get down at the next turn,' I asked.

'But we're heading right,' she said.

I smiled. 'Could you give me your diary? I want to write a book.'

She hesitated. 'It's personal… but fine. Come with me. I want to know you before handing it over.'

I got into the auto with her. We reached a café, where I showed her my books—*Forest Sentinel* and *Hurt, Heal, Growth*.

She flipped through them, then sighed.

'Actually,' she said, 'I was bringing this diary from Jannaram to my hometown, Kochi. It's not meant for a book—it's a personal diary.'

I looked at her. 'Please, let me turn it into a book. I'll do justice to it.'

I told her everything—about my writing, about my books, about why this diary meant something to me.

After a long pause, she finally nodded. 'Fine.'

I took the diary, reached home, rested on my bed, and opened it.

And that's where it all began.

I'm Vikram, I hope Anika finds this book.

The sun was bright, just like summer. Well, summer had just ended. It's June. And just like June, things are pretty bad for a guy like me. It's the month when schools reopen. I had been playing cricket almost every day—it's just like having a lot of passion for it. The way I hit fours, the way I solely led the matches to victory.

Here I am, in a stationery shop, buying a notebook that will be used for just ten days.

'Uncle, long notebook,' I asked as I entered the shop. He showed me two options—one with a Justin Bieber cover, with a completely white paper back, and the other with creamy paper. I preferred the creamy one. And I additionally bargained for a Virat Kohli poster. He demanded 100 bucks for it but I got it for twenty. While walking home, I saw my father twice. He crossed my way on his bike, his sharp eyes making me feel terrible. He's a uniformed officer. Like every guy whose father is a cop or in the civil services, the son must be an innocent soul. But not in my case. I had another world waiting for me when

I entered my room.

I opened the door to my room, which was filled with books on all sides, a cricket bat in one corner and wires all over my table as my next project was making a drone. I placed the stationery on the table, took some tape,

and pasted Virat Kohli's poster between Eminem, Michael Jackson and Dostoevsky's portraits.

I went to my mom—she was watching a TV serial. I quietly laid my head on her lap, and in no time, I fell asleep.

The Following Day

My mom woke me up and made me get ready for school, which was too boring for me—boring friends, boring lectures.

As it was the first day, I went to my class, greeted my old friends and sat on the bench. Everyone was shouting—some talking about their summer adventures, some discussing their summer vacation as it was the first day they were meeting friends after the summer vacations. But I was silent. That's who I am. I don't like to talk to people or share my things with them.

Then, an attendant came in and asked, 'Who is Vikram here?'

I wasn't really in class, though my body was present. I was lost in a Chetan Bhagat novel I had started yesterday. My friend pushed me to stand, and I stood up.

'So, you are Vikram?'

'Yes, brother,' I spoke coldly, as I usually do with everyone.

'Can't you take it after class?'

'Why should I?' I asked. 'You're the CR, right?'

The new session had just started—how could someone become a CR without attending classes of given exams?

Everyone in the class thought it was a joke and laughed. I looked around, wondering what made them laugh.

'Shut up!' the attendant said.

'You were first in the last fourth finals, right?' he asked. 'I don't remember,' I said, rubbing my head in confusion.

'You are. Handle the class, or else you'll be punished,' he said, then came closer and pinched my arm hard. But I didn't show any discomfort. He looked shocked and walked out.

I stood up, went near the board, and took a piece of chalk. Suddenly the class became silent.

I sat on the chair, feeling bored.

The bell rang, and I left for home with emptiness in my mind.

I reached home, hugged my mom, and went to my room, where I resumed reading *Half Girlfriend*.

The Following Day

I reached school late. I got there after the prayer. The first period had already started. As I walked through the corridors, I crossed every classroom, hearing lectures in progress.

The school was a two-storey building. Half of it was still under construction, and the unfinished parts hadn't been painted yet. The sounds of the classes hit my ears.

'May I come in, sir?' I asked while entering the class.

As I said that, my face suddenly turned to the left.

I froze for a while.

A girl. She was a newcomer.

Her eyes—captivating diamonds.

She smiled at me, even though she didn't know me.

I was still gazing at her while the whole class looked at me.

I was in a trance. I couldn't recount what was happening to me.

I felt like I was watching a goddess in her. 'Vikram!' the teacher shouted. 'Come in.'

I quickly averted my gaze and sat on the last bench, surrounded by boring people.

The bell rang. I looked at her—her skin was glowing. I don't usually have any interest in humans, but I don't know why…I felt close to her within the blink of an eye. I wished I could have stared at her face all day.

I went to the washroom. As I came back, my friend had already started talking to her. I averted my gaze towards the bench.

The teacher left. The class became violent again.

I went near the board and picked up a piece of chalk.

Her eyes slowed down my movement. My gaze shifted to the other side, but I was struck by her eyes again. I stared at her for a minute, then quickly felt annoyed and averted my gaze.

The attendant came in.

'Vikram, please come to the office. Your father has arrived.'

My heart started to pound the moment I heard it. My father? In the middle of a school day?

What did he come for? Was it a complaint or something else?

I was terrified. My father barely came to school, not even for my admission or to pay the tuition fee.

I slowly walked down the stairs and entered the principal's office. I saw my father and walked closer to him.

The principal spoke.

'Vikram, your grandfather has passed away. Your father came to pick you up.'

It sounded normal to me.

I didn't know why, but my father looked heartbroken.

I accompanied him on his bike, and we reached home.

My grandfather lived in a village 200 kilometres away from our town.

We travelled in a car through vast farmlands. The village looked like something straight out of the '90s.

Men were spinning pottery wheels. Women were picking clothes from the drying areas. A few men stood on the roadside, smoking sutta. As the car entered the village, we saw a huge banyan tree come into view in the centre. Some men were sitting under it drinking a whitish local brew on teak leaves.

As we reached home, a crowd had gathered, waiting for my father. Being the eldest, he had to take care of everything.

16

As soon as my father got out of the vehicle, the entire gathering ran towards him as if they were welcoming a celebrity. I got out too and looked around for a seat. As soon as I spotted one, I rushed over and sat down.

I pulled *Half Girlfriend* out from under my jacket and started reading.

Unfortunately, my chair was right next to my grandfather's dead body.

Everyone turned and looked at me with annoyed expressions. Some stopped crying. Some whispered amongst themselves.

My sister ran towards me, snatched the book from my hands, and slapped me across the face.

I didn't react. I was still holding the story in my mind.

I looked up and saw my father crying loudly.

I had never seen him this weak. I didn't go near him. My mother and sister were crying near the dead body,

but I didn't join them. Instead, I observed the women under the tent.

Some were crying for sympathy. Some were hiding their faces with sarees, avoiding showing their emotions.

The Following Day

'Mom, when are we leaving this place?'

'After eleven days of your grandfather's death,' she replied. 'Mom, that's too much! What will I do here? I am bored. Amma, I'll go to Karimnagar with Babai.'

'No! You have to stay here! You don't even have the right to leave the house. Stay until the eleventh day.'

'But what do I do here? It's too boring!'

'You have so many cousins. Why don't you play with them?'

How could I tell my mom that I had lost interest in human contact?

Every time I tried to be friends with someone, I ended up feeling isolated—even when surrounded by people. My mind was always elsewhere, constantly meandering through different paths.

I lay on my bed and took a nap.

My brain was flooded with memories—the girl I had seen at school.

Who was she? Why had she chosen that school? What was the reason behind her smile? And why was I getting signs of love from her? What was I supposed to do with these memories?

A dream swept over me.

We were in a park, talking about Howard Roark, Ayn Rand, and many other things. She was just listening, smiling.

I suddenly woke up, confused, and slapped myself five times.

'Dude, why am I getting trapped in her trance? What is happening to me? Why am I like this?'

My cousins saw me and started laughing for no reason.

I smiled back and lay down again.

But I couldn't sleep. Her memories kept coming back to me.

I started dreaming about her, even though I knew I shouldn't.

Five days passed.

Her memories haunted me badly.

I couldn't take it anymore. I grabbed my phone and dialled Madhukar.

'Hello! Madhu!'

'Yeah, Vikram. How are you?'

'I'm good. Dude, can I ask you a question?' 'Yeah, Vikram.'

'Who's that new girl?' 'Who? A lot of girls joined.' 'The girl in the last bench.' 'Oh, Anika!'

I didn't know her name, but she might be the one.

Madhu laughed. 'What's the matter, dude? I've never seen you ask about a girl before.'

I smiled. 'No reason. Just asking.' 'Have you fallen in love?'

I wanted to say yes.

But instead, I said, 'No, I'm not interested.'

'Don't even try, dude. Mukesh is getting close to her, and she seems to be talking to him nicely.'

My heart felt like it was carrying a ton of weight.

Something shifted inside me.

I felt different, like a heartbroken guy.

'Hmm. Good,' I replied, forcing myself to sound indifferent.

'You want to know anything else?'

'No, dude. Just wanted to talk. How's uncle and aunt?'

'They're good.'

'Okay. Bye.'

'Yeah, bye.'

I wasn't able to bear the pain. I should have been there. This funeral made me miss my chance.

My life has always been like this—just unlucky.

TWO

CLASS V

The last six days felt like the hardest period of my life. It was as though I was heartbroken, even though I hadn't been in a relationship with her. I couldn't escape her memories. They clung to me, like an invisible weight I couldn't shed.

I was climbing the stairs when I suddenly came face-to-face with her. As she descended, my heart was overwhelmed by her smile. Her eyes were sharp, and I felt like a liquid poured over my body, freezing me in place.

I entered the class and saw Mukesh sitting beside me. How could I tell him that I had a crush on Anika? No way. What if he told her? I had to keep my composure and try to move on. But every time I did, it felt like I was losing something important.

Then she entered the class, smiling. This time, she looked at Mukesh with that same smile, and he smiled back at her. The class teacher came in with a stack of diaries to distribute. She called Anika to pass them out. With her smile, Anika moved from one person to the next, handing out the diaries.

When she reached my bench, she gave Mukesh a diary, then looked at me for a moment. Her eyes quickly darted away, as if I were some criminal who had just been released from jail. I couldn't understand what was happening between us. I felt rejected, and it hurt deeply.

The teacher left, and since the maths teacher was absent, I was supposed to handle the next period. I grabbed a piece of chalk and walked to the board. But as I turned to face the class, everyone shouted, 'Vikram, no! Don't do that! Leave us alone.'

I turned around and said, 'Okay, what do we do then?' 'Let's play Antakshari!' someone suggested.

I protested. 'It's not possible!'

'Games? Let's go to the ground!' another person shouted.

'Do you really want to play?' I asked. 'Of course!' they all yelled.

'Someone has to join me to the staff room to get permission,' I said, but no one raised their hand. Their faces dropped until a hand suddenly shot up. It was Anika, smiling at me.

'Okay, let's go!' I said, heading for the door.

Just then, Mukesh approached us. 'I'm coming with you too.'

My heart raced, but I didn't show it. He joined us as we walked out.

They were whispering and laughing behind me, and my anxiety shot through the roof. Had they fallen in love? My heart sank. This was my unfortunate fate.

I reached the staff room, and suddenly, Anika grabbed my hand, pulling me to a stop.

'What?' I turned to her.

'See there,' she whispered, closing her mouth with her hands. Her voice, so innocent and soft, tugged at my heart. She pointed towards the window.

I peered through, and my eyes widened. There, our PT teacher and a teacher were kissing each other. They saw us too. The PT teacher rushed towards us.

'What are you both doing here?' he asked, his voice sharp.

Mukesh, seeing the situation, quickly bolted away. I nervously explained, 'Sir, we had a break, and we thought we'd play a game.'

'Okay, go play,' he grumbled, still not fully convinced.

'Thank you, sir,' I muttered, trying to keep my composure.

'Did you see anything?' he asked, his eyes narrowing.

'No, sir, I was just saying—'

'Yes, you were helping madam clear her throat, right?' Anika said.

'What?' I thought to myself, my heart racing.

23

The teacher hurried over to us. 'He might've just been helping me out. I ate some fish, and... well...' she trailed off, clearly trying to cover up.

I was at a loss for words. '*How could anyone even say that?*' I thought.

'Just forget it, sir,' I said, my voice shaking slightly.

'If you tell anyone what you saw, I'll suspend both of you,' the sir threatened, glaring at us.

'Sure, sir,' I said quickly, eager to get out of there. We left the staff room and headed towards the class.

'Vikram, what brand is your watch?' Anika suddenly asked.

'It's a Titan,' I muttered under my breath, 'None of your business.' I snapped, and she quickly shut up.

Back in class, the news of permission given to play games spread like wildfire. Everyone started shouting and pushing each other around. I was shoved to the ground. Anika placed her hand on Mukesh's shoulder and walked away.

I stood there, feeling alone. I loved being alone, but this time, my mind couldn't stop thinking about her. Why? I didn't know, but the thoughts about her were relentless. I left the room and headed towards the ground.

I saw Mukesh and Anika playing together in the sand. It felt like a punch to my chest. I didn't know how to explain to either of them what I was feeling.

Months Pass

The days felt like a nightmare. Anika and Mukesh had grown very close. Mukesh eventually confessed to me that he was in love with her. I found out she had even bought him a gift for his birthday.

Frustrated, I asked him one day, 'So, what are you planning to do, Mukesh?'

'What do you want me to do?' he replied with a shrug, as if he didn't understand my pain.

'You've got three months before the summer holidays. If you miss the chance now, she might not even be in the same school next year.'

I wanted to end the turmoil in my mind. If she accepted his proposal, at least I would be able to let go of her memory.

He smiled shyly and hugged me. 'Thank you, dude. I'm lucky to have a friend like you who always gives the best advice.'

I almost wanted to tell him—I was unlucky to have a friend like you! You're stealing my crush, you asshole! But I just smiled and said nothing.

Finally, the day arrived. It was the school's Annual Day, but for me, it felt like Independence Day. I would finally be free from her thoughts. Mukesh had prepared to propose to Anika. He brought her a shiny Dairy Milk Silk chocolate, which I had helped him buy.

'Thanks, Vikram,' he said, hugging me. 'I don't know how to thank you. I wish you'd be my friend forever.'

I smiled, but to myself, I thought, *just propose to her and get her out of my life.*

Later, I was on stage with my team, preparing for the drama performance. Anika was standing near the stairs, and I quickly avoided her gaze, not wanting to make eye contact.

'Vikram!' she called out.

'What, Anika?' I asked, trying to keep my distance. 'All the best,' she said, shaking my hand. As I held her

hand for that moment, I couldn't help but feel like those hands could one day tie a rakhi on my wrist, but I buried those thoughts.

I walked towards the stage for my performance. The drama was simple: a message about the dangers of drinking and driving. Two drunk guys start their bikes, only to get hit by a truck. They die. Then, two women—Sandeep and Ajay, wearing sarees—came to mourn their loss. Ajay, though, had trouble with his saree; he only wore it on the top without any shorts underneath. When I asked him why, he proudly said, 'It should be like a real wife's saree.'

The scene was supposed to depict the wives crying over their dead husbands, and I was to give a speech at the end. Everything was going according to plan until Ajay tripped over the microphone wire, and his saree flew, revealing his underwear. He didn't stop, he didn't even notice as he continued crying, fully unaware of his appearance. The entire crowd burst into laughter.

Anika caught the saree as it flew through the air and handed it to me with her eyes closed. I quickly covered Ajay up, he didn't respond—he was still in his character.

Then I walked towards the centre of the stage and gave my speech. What was supposed to be a three-line speech turned into five minutes. The audience gave me a standing ovation, though I wasn't sure if it was for my speech or the comedy caused by Ajay.

Then came the real moment—the one I had been dreading. Mukesh was about to propose to Anika. He called her into a classroom, which was like a small flat with three rooms combined. He told her he wanted to show her something.

I ran behind them, not wanting to miss a second of the moment. My classmates in the field must have thought I was up to something. But I didn't care. I hurried to the balcony to see what would happen.

I could see through the window. Anika entered, and Mukesh handed her the chocolate. She smiled as if she had already agreed.

My heart was racing uncontrollably.

'I love you, Anika,' Mukesh confessed, just like in the movies, pulling a flower from his pocket.

She froze for a moment, covering her face with her hands.

Say yes, Anika. Say yes, I whispered under my breath.

But then, Anika threw the chocolate on the floor. 'I never thought you'd speak to me like this. You're just a friend, Mukesh. I'm sorry, I can't be in love with you. You're like a brother to me.'

I was overwhelmed with emotion. For a split second, I felt like dancing with joy, but then reality hit me.

'Why were you behaving as you are close to me?' Mukesh asked, hurt.

'I thought you were just a friend. If you developed such feelings, I really can't do anything about it, okay?' She replied.

Mukesh was upset. I felt sorry for him, but I also understood how he must have felt. I went to the door, and just as I was about to leave, Anika exited the room, looking at me with confusion.

I approached Mukesh. 'What happened, man? Are you okay?'

'Yeah, why are you here, Vikram?' he asked, trying to act normal, but I could see the sadness in his eyes.

'I was curious about your proposal, dude,' I said, pointing to the chocolate lying on the ground. 'Is that all you have to say?'

'Nope,' he answered flatly.

'What's next?' I asked, trying to lighten the mood. 'Dude, chill. There are millions of girls out there,' he said, trying to cheer up.

I left the room and walked towards the ground, feeling a strange sense of joy mixed with relief. I didn't know why.

CLASS V

The summer heat was unbearable. With temperatures soaring above 50°C, I was stuck inside, looking for comfort in novels. I had collected every Chetan Bhagat book I could find and had already read most of them, trying to escape all thoughts of Anika.

'Vikram, try to find some carrots,' my mom called out as we wandered through the crowded local market. The place resembled a playground, surrounded by vendors selling vegetables.

I was making my way through the stalls when I bumped into someone. Looking up, I saw it was Anika, walking alongside her mother.

Anika smiled, and I gave her my awkward lopsided grin in return.

I returned home and found myself daydreaming again. I imagined Anika in a field surrounded by flowers, with the song '*Nenjukkul Peidhidum*' playing softly in the background. Every day, I found myself thinking about her, even though I knew I shouldn't. Her thoughts had completely consumed me, and I wasn't sure how to get rid of them. The more I tried, the harder it became.

But I couldn't stop. My mind was set on one thing—I had to settle down and marry her.

Suddenly, my phone beeped. It was a message from Bittu, a senior in my colony.

'Hey, bro, come to the ground. Let's play cricket.'

I quickly replied, cutting the message short. I headed to the ground, knowing that when a senior calls for a game, it usually means they need fielders. I hadn't played cricket in a month, but fielding was my strength. I didn't care if I didn't get to bowl or bat—I just loved being out there.

The match was between our Vidya Nagar colony and the Sri Lanka colony. We won the toss and decided to bowl first. They set a target of 70 runs in 10 overs, which was tough for anyone in our locality to achieve.

Our batting was a disaster. By the time we had faced five overs, we were 5 wickets down with just 25 runs on the board. The tension was palpable.

But then, it was my turn. I took the bat with a heavy heart. Everyone had lost hope, but I tried to keep the spirits high. I commanded the strike to rotate, but when it was my turn to face the bowler, the situation looked bleak.

The bowler delivered a fast ball, and I tried to defend it, but I missed. The ball nearly hit the stumps. Everyone was disappointed, and the mood was grim. We knew we had probably lost the match.

The bowler threw the second ball—a bouncer. I had no clue how to tackle it, so I instinctively bent my head down. Our captain was about to give up on us, but the opposition captain intervened, suggesting we play until the last over.

I stayed silent. Holding my bat, I focused, watched the ball carefully, and with all my strength, I hit it. The ball soared and flew over the boundary for a six. For a brief moment, everything stopped. The entire field was silent as they all stared in disbelief. Even our captain stood there, mouth agape, unable to process the distance of the shot. No one had ever hit a six like that in our colony.

The bowler threw the fourth ball, and it was even faster than before. I managed to knock it and rotate the strike, giving my teammate a chance to play.

Two overs left. We needed 42 runs. The team's mood wasn't great, but I could feel the adrenaline rush. The next over, I was on strike again. The first ball—another six. Then the second, and the third. The crowd, our teammates, and everyone watching were suddenly full of joy, as if they were savouring a victory. The mood had shifted from despair to hope.

At the fourth ball, I rotated the strike again. The striker missed the next two balls, but the pressure was mounting. There were only six balls left, and we needed 19 runs. Everyone was holding their breath, and even the uncles from the colony who had come to watch, had their eyes glued to the match.

The bowler came in, his expression fierce, clearly intent on taking me down. I held my bat, ready for the challenge.

He bowled the first ball, and I stepped forward to hit it. The ball flew to the boundary again. The second ball came, and my bat missed it completely. The keeper ran towards the ball and caught it. I was stunned.

I walked back to the crease, watching the sad faces of my teammates and the uncles. They were all disappointed. I should have been more patient with the ball, waiting for the right opportunities. I should have held back a little longer. The last three balls could have been sixes.

Suddenly, the umpire whistled. 'No ball!' the captain shouted.

I turned to see the umpire signalling it was a no-ball because the bowler had overstepped the line.

I rushed back to my position. The umpire confirmed that it was a free hit, meaning I had another chance. The ball came in, and I closed my eyes, swinging with all my might. The ball soared again, but it was caught by the fielder. Another no-ball! I had survived.

The third ball was a dot, and the tension was unbearable. Just one ball left. We needed six runs to win. Everyone was holding their breath. My heart was pounding louder than ever.

I could see the bowler in slow motion. I closed my eyes, swung the bat as hard as I could, and prayed. When I finally opened my eyes, I realised the ball had cleared the boundary again—another six!

Our captain ran towards me, lifting me into the air, and the entire team erupted in celebration. People were shouting, hugging each other, and dancing. We had done it. We had won!

For the next few days, I became the team's opener. Every match was filled with excitement, and everyone in the colony would gather around to watch me bat. We won every game, and I scored two half-centuries in the process. The victory felt sweet, not just because of the match, but because for those brief moments, the world seemed right. All the frustration, all the pain, and all the heartaches faded away in those glorious moments on the field.

10 P.M.

I had skipped dinner, waiting for my father to return from work.

He worked in another mandal and only came home on weekends. The place where he worked didn't have a proper school for us, so he had to live away from us.

The doorbell rang.

I rushed to the hall, excitement bubbling inside me.

I opened the door, expecting something—maybe a smile, maybe a glance. But my father showed no signs of even noticing my existence.

My mother carried a hard box with his dinner and placed it on the table. I sat beside him as he ate, hoping for a moment to talk.

I didn't even greet him.

I swallowed my breath and spoke, forcing the words out. 'Daddy...'

He didn't look up.

'What?' He replied in an aggressive tone. I took a step back instantly.

'Nothing,' I said.

My mother, understanding my hesitation, spoke for me. 'He wants a bat and ball,' she said. 'He wants to play cricket with his friends. Since no one has a bat, he wants to buy one and play with them.'

My father kept eating. 'So why are you asking me?'
'Money', my mother said.

He stopped chewing. 'Let him earn the money he wants. I can only pay for his studies.'

My mother sighed. 'He really loves cricket. The entire colony is talking about how well he plays. He might have a future in it. Why don't we let him try?'

Suddenly, my father slammed his fist against the dining table.

The impact made the plates rattle, and food scattered across the surface.

His voice thundered. 'He has to study hard and get a good job! My parents didn't make me study. I have struggled with this odd job enough—I don't want him to go through the same!'

I froze.

My mother placed a hand on my shoulder. 'What if he has a career in cricket?

Don't worry, Chinna, I'll buy you one.'

My father left his plate and stormed into his room, slamming the door shut.

Her words gave me a sense of relief, but still, the question lingered in my mind: Was my father right? Should I follow his path and focus only on my studies, or was there really a future for me in cricket? It was a battle between my love for the game and the weight of my father's expectations.

Summer passed, and with it came the most exciting days of the year. The whole colony continued talking about my batting skills, and Sandeep and I spent hours perfecting our game. The summer heat didn't matter; nothing could take away the joy I felt when I was on the field, bat in hand, ready to face any challenge that came my way.

But June came too soon, and with it, school started again. The excitement of the summer game gave way to the routine of classes, homework, and the pressure of what was expected of me. Every time I picked up my books, my mind wandered to the field, to the sound of the ball hitting the bat, and to the dreams I had of playing cricket for real.

I was the first to arrive at school that morning. I kept wondering about Anika.

The school started at 9, but time moved painfully slow. My eyes were glued to the entrance, waiting, hoping. But what if she had changed to a different school?

One by one, students arrived, carrying their notebooks. But Anika didn't.

As days passed, disappointment crept in.

After school, I asked one of her friends about her absence. The reply shattered my hope.

'She might have changed school. We didn't have much contact with her.'

That night, I convinced myself with a hopeful thought—
She'll come tomorrow.

But the next day, she didn't.

After a Week

My anxiety was unbearable. Where had she gone?

I wrote down the names of all the schools in our area
and started asking my mutual friends if they had seen her.
One after another, the answer was the same—No.

Then, I made my final call. My last and only hope—
one of the most well-known schools in Jannaram.

'Hey, Sai!'

'Vikram! How are you?'

'I'm good. Can I ask you something? 'Yeah, what's up?'

'Did any new girl join your class?'

'Yeah, quite a few.'

'Anyone from our school?'

There was a pause. He murmured for a second. 'Yeah,
I think there's one.'

My heart pounded. 'What's her name?' I jumped from
my chair.

'Not sure, dude. Why?'

'Try to find out tomorrow!'

I ended the call and rushed to my mom. 'Mom, I feel
exhausted.'

She looked up. 'What happened?'

'I want to change schools. It's boring here. The teachers aren't great. I want to transfer to Slate High School.'

She sighed. 'We tried to enrol you there before, but you chose this school instead. I'm thankful you've finally changed your decision. I'll call your dad and check his schedule. I will ask him to come, if he can, and get you transferred tomorrow itself.'

I hugged her.

The Following Day

I went to class to say goodbye to my friends.

Some looked emotional (probably because they could copy from me in exams). Others looked happy (finally they could take the first rank).

Then I walked into the staff room for the final step— signing the transfer papers.

My father was sitting across from the principal, who was trying to convince him to reconsider my transfer. But my father didn't budge.

I stepped forward. He handed me a pen.

All eyes were on me, waiting, watching. It felt like I was signing an autograph.

Just as I was about to sign, an old ringtone played on a teacher's phone.

Then, a voice hit my ears.

'May I come in, sir?'

I froze.

That voice.

I turned my head instantly. It was Anika.

She stood there in a white T-shirt, the gold of her earrings shining. Her smile was breathtaking.

She walked in with her father. My heart almost stopped. 'Anika, where were you all this time?' a teacher asked. 'Sir, we were in Tirupati.'

A wave of shock ran through me. She hadn't transferred. She hadn't left. She was here all along.

My hands started shaking. Sweat trickled down my face. 'Make it quick,' my father said in a stern tone.

My throat went dry. 'Dad...' I struggled to speak. 'What?'

I swallowed hard. 'I'll go next year. I want to study here this year.' My heartbeat raced.

'No. Sign the document. I've already paid the advance. We have to move.' His voice grew sharp.

I closed my eyes for a second and silently prayed. Then his phone rang.

He stepped outside to take the call.

The principal leaned in. 'Vikram, why are you so confused? You're such a bright student. Just tell me what's wrong.'

I wanted to that I loved Anika and wanted to be near her; I was attracted to her, and her presence had unknowingly dictated my choices. But instead, I simply said, 'Nothing, sir.'

The principal sighed. 'What do you want to do now?'

I looked down. 'It's not in my hands, sir. It's my father's decision.'

At that moment, my father re-entered the room. He had heard my last sentence.

Parents always say they give us freedom to choose, but in reality, they make the choices for us.

He walked towards me and looked into my eyes.

Then, in a calm voice, he said, 'Do what you want to do. I am with you.'

THREE

ANIKA

~

As the class began, I sat at my desk, trying to focus on what the teacher was saying, but my thoughts kept drifting back to Anika. Her smile, the way she had entered the room so confidently, everything about her seemed to captivate me. It was as if time had paused for those few moments when our eyes had met, and now, the world felt like it was finally returning to some semblance of order. Yet, I couldn't shake the nagging feeling of uncertainty.

What if things had changed between us? What if Mukesh had gotten closer to her again?

I glanced at her, but this time, I kept my distance. She was busy listening to the teacher, just like everyone else. There was no sign of the old closeness we had shared, but that didn't stop my heart from racing every time she glanced in my direction.

The minutes seemed to stretch on forever. I kept looking at the clock, waiting for the bell to ring, for the class to be over, so I could have a chance to talk to her. But the teacher's voice was steady, filling the air, while my mind was filled with questions I didn't know how to ask.

Finally, the bell rang signalling a break. I packed my bag slowly, my hands trembling as I looked around, trying to gather the courage to go and speak to her. As I made my way out of the classroom, I noticed her standing by the window, talking to a couple of friends. She looked calm, composed, and completely at ease. I wondered if she was still thinking about what had happened before.

I took a deep breath and walked towards her, unsure of what to say. As I got closer, she looked up at me and her expression softened. 'Hey, Vikram,' she said with a casual smile, but my heart was completely attracted to her. But her voice—there was something different about it. It wasn't the same warmth that I had imagined before. She seemed distant, as if the connection we once had had faded into something unspoken.

'Hey, Anika,' I replied, trying to keep my voice steady. 'How've you been?'

'I'm good,' she answered quickly. There was a slight pause, and then she added, 'I heard you were transferring to another school. Why are you back?'

I hesitated for a moment, unsure of how much to share with her. But then I realised that there was no point in hiding my feelings anymore. 'I was... I was going to transfer, but then my dad changed his mind. He thought I should stay here.'

She nodded, her expression unreadable. 'I see.'

The silence between us felt heavy, but I didn't know how to break it. The words I wanted to say were stuck in my throat. Should I tell her how much I missed her, how I had been hoping to see her again? Should I tell her about everything I had been thinking while she was away?

Before I could say anything, Mukesh walked up behind us, grinning. 'Hey Vikram, glad to see you're back!' he said, as if he hadn't just been part of the whirlwind of emotions I was going through.

I forced a smile, but inside, I felt a knot tighten in my stomach. In the past, Mukesh had always been close to Anika. I wondered if anything had changed while she was away. Would he be the one to fill the space I thought I had in her life?

Anika smiled casually at Mukesh as if nothing had happened, but then quickly turned to me. 'Well, I'll catch up with you guys later,' she said before walking away with her friends, leaving me standing there, feeling lost in my thoughts.

I stood there for a moment, watching her leave, trying to make sense of everything that had happened. The doubts, the questions, the uncertainty—it all swirled around me, and I knew that this was only the beginning of figuring out where I stood with her.

But for now, I had to focus on the present. I had returned to school, and maybe, just maybe, I could find my way back to Anika. I wasn't sure how or when, but I knew one thing for sure—this wasn't the end. It was just the start of a new chapter.

The school bell rang as everyone rushed out of the class to the ground.

Anika started playing kabaddi along with the other girls in her class.

I sat on a chair and started staring at her. She was impressive in terms of sports. When the last period bell rang, everybody moved towards Anika's kabaddi game, as it was the sports period.

Shashi dragged my hand. 'Where?'

'Upstairs.' 'Why?'

'Just follow me.'

We headed upstairs and entered our classroom verandah. Shashi picked up a piece of rock from the ground before we went up.

'What are we going to do now?'

'Let's hit that honeybee nest.'

'Are you out of your mind, dude?'

'Yeah, let's do it!'

'But why?'

'For fun, simple!'

'You've gone mad! I'm getting away—' Before I could finish my sentence, he hurled the stone at the nest. The honeybees swarmed out in a frenzy, scattering everywhere. He grabbed my hand, and we bolted down the stairs.

Everyone stared at us as the entire swarm of honeybees chased us. We ran for our lives. Finally, they left us.

I stopped running and found myself standing in the kabaddi ground beside Anika. She saw me and started scolding me.

'What if those honeybees had stung you? Stupid! Don't you have any sense?'

She began checking my body to see if any bees were left, patting my back. 'Huff… nothing's there,' she said in relief. She placed a finger on her lips, observing me closely with her pretty face.

'Why are you even smiling?' she asked.

I kept smiling because of her, ignoring her words. 'He's gone mad,' Priya remarked.

'Vikram, are you okay?' She placed her hand on my shoulder and tapped me.

'Yeah… yeah,' I giggled. Then I noticed everyone surrounding us. The PT sir ran towards us.

'Who did that?' he demanded.

I was about to confess, but Anika stepped forward and spoke, 'Sir, they just swarmed out suddenly. It wasn't his fault.'

When a girl stands up for a boy, the feeling is truly special, beyond words!

Like someone trying to impress his crush through his attire, I wore a nice black tee with white sleeves and paired it with sneakers.

Sunday Class

We had class although it was a Sunday.

I reached the classroom but no one was there yet. I waited for two hours until I saw an auto entering the school campus. Six girls, including Anika, got out and walked in. I watched from the top of the school building like a guy holding a pair of binoculars.

They entered the class, but I sat at my bench, pretending they didn't exist.

'Hey, Vikram,' one girl, Shruti, spoke.

'Yeah, Shruti?' I responded as if I were normal, though I was feeling very anxious.

'Do we have class today?'

'I don't know.'

I was staring at Anika this time. She had applied lipstick and had placed a finger over her lips, looking at somewhere in the distance.

'What do we do now?' Anika asked, disappointment clear on her face. She was too cute.

'I have my mobile. Let me dial Anil sir.'

I took out my phone, went to the balcony, and faked a call.

Anil sir 'instructed' us to go to the projection lab and solve every problem in Exercise 5.2. He would arrive in half an hour.

The girls panicked when they heard about the exercise. 'Let's go,' Anika said, dragging them to the lab.

Four of the girls sat in groups and started solving the problems. Anika placed her pencil on her lips.

'Hey girls, I've solved every one of them. Here you go,' I said, handing them my notes.

Basically, I had solved every exercise from the book during the summer. I didn't have any major work to do, except cricket, so I picked up every book and completed everything.

'Thank you!' They took my book instantly and copied everything in five minutes.

'Done!' Anika said and stood up.

The lab was a 7x7 square-foot room, with one end covered by a curtain.

Anika walked towards it.

There's a saying: *Don't follow girls, follow dreams. But for me, the girl was the dream.* So I followed.

I lifted the curtain and entered. She was sitting there, holding a boat made from scrap materials. She read the words written on it aloud:

'By Vikram.'

She turned back, shocked to see me.

'You did this?' she asked with a cute expression.

'Yeah!'

'This is so cool!' Her eyes wandered to another side. She dug her hands into the pile of scrap again. This time, she pulled out a drone.

'Vikram too?'

'You're really cool, Vikram! You made this?' 'Nah, it's not finished yet. I left it halfway.'

'Why?'

'I'm not sure I can do it.'

'Why not try again?'

When those words come from your crush, no matter how difficult the task, you have to do it.

I smiled. She smiled. She took both the boat and the drone and sat down. Then, she called me closer.

I was an introvert, suddenly hit by a storm of anxiety. 'Come on, Vikram!' she called again.

I walked in and sat a foot away from her. But she quickly scooted closer until our legs touched.

I explained how I built those things—how I structured the body, attached motors, connected the motherboard, and programmed them. She listened with fascination, her eyes soaking in every detail. Then, as she leaned in to examine the drone, she unknowingly moved even closer.

We were so close that if either of us moved an inch, our bodies would touch.

'Dude,' she muttered, suddenly turning her face towards me.

I instinctively turned mine too. Our lips brushed.

She pushed me away and ran out.

I sat there in a trance. I had no idea what had just happened.

I didn't leave immediately. I stayed there for ten minutes before finally stepping out from behind the curtain.

The four girls were cracking jokes and laughing with each other.

As I entered, Anika turned her face away.

I sat beside them and tried to talk to her, but every time I did, she dismissed me.

The Following Day

I went to school and saw her. She glanced at me once with a serious face and then turned away.

Seven days passed. I kept trying to start a conversation, but she ignored me every time.

I returned home, thinking about everything that had happened.

Finally, I made a decision—I had to move away from her. For the next month, I tried to focus on my studies, but I couldn't get her out of my mind. The first-semester exams were approaching, and everyone was busy preparing.

A Day Before the Exam

I was walking out of the class, spinning my pen around my finger, when suddenly a senior entered with a flower in his hand.

I stopped and looked back.

There were four girls standing behind him—Anika in the middle.

She was looking straight at me. My heart started pounding.

The senior walked up to her and handed her the rose in a proposal.

My pen slipped from my fingers and clattered to the floor. The sudden sound drew everyone's attention towards me.

Anika stared at me with a serious expression.

I quickly walked away to give them privacy and waited at the far end of the classroom.

The senior left the class with a happy face. I was heartbroken.

And then came the words that shattered me— 'She accepted.'

My heart broke into a million pieces.

I didn't know why, but I couldn't cry, couldn't laugh—I couldn't do anything.

I buried my pain deep inside and focused on my semester exams.

The results were out. I had secured the first rank. Anika was second.

The room filled with applause. She laughed. I felt uncomfortable standing beside her. How I wish I could delete that lab scene from my memory.

Dussehra was one of the most celebrated festivals in Telangana. We had fifteen days off.

Fifteen days during which I wouldn't see Anika.

For nine days, women celebrated Bathukamma—a festival where flowers are decorated into a cone shape and placed on a plate. Women bring their bathukammas to the community centre and dance in circles around them.

I spent most of my time playing cricket.

One Evening

'Sandeep, I want to see Anika,' I said.

'Why are you so interested in that girl?'

'I don't know.'

'But she's already committed to that senior.'

'Yeah, but… I don't know, man. I just want to see her. Do you have a solution?'

'Anika's house is 20 kilometres from here, dude.'

'Twenty? My God! My parents won't allow that,' I said, sitting on a bench near the community centre.

'And if you want to see her, we have to go at night. Not in the morning.'

'My God. Night? Sandeep, they won't even permit me in the morning, and now you're talking about sneaking out at night? How is that even possible?'

'It has to be. There's no other way.' 'Okay… but how do we go there?'

'I'll bring my father's bike,' Sandeep said. 'Really? How will your father allow that?'

'I'll tell him I'm going to your house. He'll definitely agree if you're involved.'

'How should we convince my parents?'

'Tell your parents that you're coming to my house for a movie. Or games.'

'I have a PlayStation at home. But how will they believe that and send me over?'

'But you don't have the remote.'

'But I had it, right?'

'It will go missing, no?'

'How could it go missing?'

'You dumbhead! How do I even explain it to you?' he exclaimed, placing his hands on his head.

'Don't worry, we'll plan something,' he replied calmly

'Okay, dude, we'll see.'

'We have to do this. There's no other way.'

I convinced my parents, and Sandeep convinced his. We both got on the bike and headed toward her village.

'Hey dude, do you love her?' Sandeep asked while driving.

'I don't know, dude.'

'You do!'

'How could I fall in love?'

'See, we're risking our lives and heading towards her house. That's what everyone calls love.'

'How?'

'Risking your life for someone is love!'

'You mean... I love her?'

'Yeah! Just tell me, shall we go back?'

'Why, dude?'

'Look at your scared face! You love her. It's time to admit it.'

'But... she has a boyfriend.'

'Do you want to kick him out and steal her love?'

'I wish I could... but she might be happy with him. Let her be.'

'Then what about you?'

'I have my books. I remember what my mother told me in childhood—*Love books, they'll give you knowledge. Love a girl, and it will give you pain.* I should have fed that into my mind, but unfortunately, I deserve this.'

We reached her village. My heart was pounding hard, and my breath grew heavier with every step.

'Do you know her house?' I asked Sandeep as he navigated through an unfamiliar direction.

'Yeah.'

'Dude, I'm scared. Should we cancel this?'

'Nah, we're almost there! Don't worry. Here we are— this is where she lives.'

As we entered, a group of boys stood at the entrance, looking at us suspiciously.

'Dude, there she is!'

Sandeep raised his finger to point at a girl. I saw her.

My heartbeat raced. It was her. I was finally seeing her after so long.

My face broke into a smile.

And then...

The senior entered on his bike. She looked at him and smiled.

Sandeep watched the scene unfold and silently turned the bike towards the Godavari river.

'Dude, calm down,' he said.

My eyes were almost overflowing.

'It's just a girl. Why are you getting so emotional? I've never seen you this weak in my life. Man, what's wrong with you?'

'In my otherwise depressing life, I found hope to hold onto... but I never thought that hope would belong to someone else.'

Sandeep half-hugged me. 'Vikram, calm down.'

I hugged him back and cried as loudly as I could.

FOUR

A NEW YEAR

~

The days felt endlessly long. I couldn't bring myself to read a novel or even go out to play cricket. My mother grew suspicious of my change in behaviour, but with my father away for training, there was no one to question me further. I spent my days alone in my room, unable to escape the memories of her. Sandeep tried countless ways to pull me out, but I rejected every single attempt.

School had started, but I couldn't switch schools—not because I didn't have a choice, but because I lacked the courage to stand by my decision. Now, I had to face the painful reality of witnessing Anika's love story unfold in front of me. *The hardest part of a man's life isn't finding a job—it's accepting that the girl he loves belongs to someone else.* I returned to class fi   days after school had started.

As I was about to step inside, Anika appeared in front of me.

A NEW YEAR

'Vikram! How are you? You haven't been to school these past days.'

My throat tightened, and my eyes stung. My voice came out weak.

'Nothing... just like that,' I replied.

'You don't sound okay,' she said, frowning. She reached out and touched my cheek with her forefinger. 'Oh my God! You seem to have a high fever.'

'Yeah,' I lied. The truth was, I had cried all night, and the exhaustion had spiked my body temperature.

'Take some rest, Vikram. If you need anything, just let me know...'

'Yeah, sure,' I whispered before stepping into the classroom.

'Vikram! Take charge of the class,' the math teacher instructed before stepping out to attend a phone call.

Anika's eyes sparkled with excitement. The moment the teacher left, she turned towards me.

'Vikram, we wanted to play chess.' 'Yeah, of course, Anika,' I replied.

She brought a chessboard from the staff room and started playing one-on-one matches with our classmates. She won five games in a row. Her focus was unshakeable— her eyes locked onto the chessboard, ears deaf to the noise around her.

After her fifth victory, she turned to me. 'Vikram, do you want to play?'

The entire class burst into laughter.

'Are you serious? You think you can beat Vikram?' someone shouted.

'Why not?' Anika raised an eyebrow.

'You'll never win against him in chess—that's a bet!' a guy challenged.

'Then let's bet together!' a girl added. 'I'll be on Anika's side!'

'I'm betting on Vikram!' one of my friends said. 'What's the bet?' someone asked.

'If Vikram wins, I will distribute thirty chocolates to all the boys,' the girl said.

The boys erupted in cheers.

'If Anika wins, I'll buy twenty-seven Dairy Milk chocolates for the girls,' Vikram's friend said.

Excitement filled the classroom as everyone cleared the benches and sat in a circle on the floor, eyes frozen on the chessboard.

I made my first move. A few moves in, Anika managed to take down my queen.

The girls cheered loudly, while the guy who had bet on me looked pale.

I stayed focused. In just three more moves using my knight and rook, I trapped her king—Checkmate.

The entire class of boys erupted in loud cheers.

'Wait!' the girl on Anika's side protested. 'Let them play again! If Anika loses this time, I'll personally buy chocolates for everyone!'

We played again. This time, I won in just five moves.

Then again. And again. Three consecutive wins.

The girls looked crushed, their excitement fading into disappointment. Anika sat still, unable to process the losses.

'Well… I'll buy chocolates for everyone,' she finally said, looking at her friends' disappointed faces.

'No,' I interrupted. 'I will.'

Later, I bought a big box of Dairy Milk chocolates and distributed them to everyone.

Eighth Grade

After eighth grade began, a few months passed without me speaking to Anika, nor did she speak to me. Yet, the gossip about me reached her ears every single day, because of Venkataramana.

I stopped bothering about the gossip or things beyond my control.

Chess was my best bet to get closer to Anika. Gradually, I started playing chess with Anika more often. We played almost ten games, but she never managed to defeat me. Every time we played, her eyes remained glued to the chessboard, while mine stayed fixed on her face. Sometimes, when I took too long to make a move, she would glance at me—only to catch me staring. And when she realised it, she would smile.

As days passed, Anika and I grew closer. But as the saying goes, every action has an equal and opposite reaction.

One day, I brought my drone to school and showed it to Anika.

'This is amazing!' she exclaimed. 'You have to make it fly!'

'I will. I'll try my best.'

A few days later, we were in the midst of the final exams. It was our sixth exam. Everything was going smoothly for me, Venkataramana, who sat behind me. The way I wrote my answers, the way he copied them—it was almost identical.

When the results were about to be announced, all the teachers entered the class with our answer sheets in hand. One by one, they started pointing at us. Everyone knew I was the guy behind his suspiciously crisp answers.

Soon, the news reached the principal's office. He summoned both of us regarding the alleged mass copying. Venkataramana literally begged me not to say anything. I reassured him—I wasn't the type to betray a friend.

We stood outside the principal's office, tension thick in the air. The principal looked furious, his blood pressure probably shooting through the roof.

'Come in,' he commanded.

We stepped inside his chamber. Behind him, the school's name was neatly carved into a wooden plaque, and national flags stood proudly behind him. His desk was cluttered with stacks of papers, *bona fide* certificates, and TC books. But right in front of him, placed deliberately, were our answer sheets.

A NEW YEAR

Lifting the papers in both hands, he stared at us. Our hearts nearly stopped. Venkataramana was visibly shaking. 'Venkataramana, did you copy from Vikram?' he asked.

'No,' Venkataramana replied immediately.

The principal circled around me, tapping a wooden stick against his palm.

'Don't lie. Vikram, did you show him your paper?' I took a deep breath. 'No,' I said firmly.

Suddenly, he swung the stick, hitting my back. I clenched my teeth, rubbing the spot without making a sound.

Then, he picked up Venkataramana's answer sheet and pointed at a particular section.

'Look at this,' he said.

It was a letter-writing question—where a letter was to be written to a friend. Vikram had written the letter to Venkataramana. Venkataramana wrote the same letter as Vikram's, word by word, including his own name!

The room fell silent.

'What do you say now, Venkataramana?' the principal asked.

Venkataramana remained silent, his face turning pale. 'And what about you, Vikram?'

I stayed quiet. The principal struck me again. I didn't flinch. But after a few more hits, the pain cracked through me, and before I could control it, the word slipped out.

'Yes,' I admitted.

The principal laughed. 'Venkataramana! Let's call your parents now and let them see what their child is truly capable of. Don't you feel ashamed for copying someone else's answers?'

He let me go but ordered Venkataramana to stay. Later that day, his parents came to the school. Right in front of them, the principal humiliated him.

The next day, Venkataramana entered the classroom red-faced, his eyes burning with anger.

During the break, Anika and I sat under a tree. 'How's your drone?' she asked.

'I haven't finished it yet.' 'Why not?'

'Do you want to see it?' 'Yeah!' she said excitedly. 'I'll bring it tomorrow.'

As I spoke, my eyes wandered across the schoolyard. I noticed Venkataramana, sitting at a distance, staring at us. But there was something different in his eyes—an unfamiliar intensity! He wanted to break me and to harm me in some way.

The bell rang, signalling the end of the break. We went back to class. As the boring lectures dragged on, I pulled out my phone and started scrolling absentmindedly.

When class ended, everyone left for lunch. I stayed behind, alone in the classroom. Feeling restless, I took out my phone and played Eminem's 'Superman' on speaker.

Suddenly, Anika rushed into the room with Venkataramana holding her hand. 'See Anika! Look what

Vikram is watching on his phone.' Her eyes landed on my phone screen—on the music video.

The moment she saw the scene—a woman undressing, the physical intimacy—it didn't matter to her that it was just a song. Anika thought I was watching porn as the woman was shown topless in the video.

She didn't say a word. She just slapped me.

And she walked out. I sat there, frozen.

Lost. Empty.

Later, Venkataramana and Anika became best friends. But the rumours about me never stopped. He would call her sister all the time, yet he was the one who kept spreading gossip about me.

To tell you something about Venkataramana—he was a strange one. He had a history. Back in seventh grade, he used to play with first-grade girls in a way that made everyone uncomfortable.

Days were passing, and there was no communication between me and Anika.

But I learned to stop caring. Some things were just out of my control.

One afternoon, Anika stood at the front of the class, addressing everyone.

'We need to plan something for the New Year,' she announced.

'Like what?' Trisha asked.

'Something adventurous,' Anika replied. 'What kind of adventure?'

'Let's sneak into the school at midnight,' a guy blurted out.

I immediately shook my head. 'No.' Everyone else shouted 'Yes!' in excitement.

'Vikram, don't come if you're not interested,' Anika said, her voice laced with sarcasm. 'I'm sure you have some important stuff to watch on your phone, right?'

Her words hit me harder than I expected. I could feel her resentment, all because of those endless rumours. By every passing second, she was growing stronger in hatred against me. Yet, I still enjoyed the moments we shared, even if they were filled with bitterness.

Everyone left, each going their own way. I stood there for a moment before deciding. I paid the school attendant some cash and got the keys.

At home, my father was sitting in the living room, watching the news. I quickly changed out of my school uniform into a fresh T-shirt and jeans, then sat beside him, ready to ask for permission.

Like any strict parent, I expected him to say no. But still, I had to try.

'Dad, I have to go to school tonight. It's New Year's Eve,' I said casually.

He looked at me seriously and, to my shock, said, 'Yeah, go then.'

I was stunned. He never let me out for parties, but this time, he just... agreed.

A NEW YEAR

Without wasting time, I grabbed my cycle and rode to school. I checked my watch—9.55 p.m. The plan was to meet at 10 p.m., but no one was there yet.

As I unlocked the school gate, I suddenly heard the sound of a bike approaching from behind. I turned to look—it was Anika. Her brother had come to drop her off. Trisha got down with her.

The bike's headlights illuminated Anika's outfit—a crisp white shirt tucked into black pants, a golden chain glinting around her neck.

She looked like an angel. No, every girl looks like an angel in that outfit, I corrected myself.

As they walked towards me, I greeted Anika. She didn't respond.

'Hey, Vikram,' Trisha spoke instead.

'What do we do? No one's here yet,' I said.

'Can't you wait?' Anika snapped, irritation evident in her tone. I shut my mouth.

She pulled out her phone and dialled someone. 'Hello, Venki...' she said, her voice suddenly soft, almost affectionate.

My blood boiled for a second, but I didn't react. She spoke briefly and cut the call.

'Venki's on the way,' she announced.

'Oh, that gay boy?' The words slipped from my mouth before I could stop them.

'Mind your tongue, Vikram,' Anika warned, her glare cutting through me.

63

I said nothing after that.

Ten minutes later, two boys and a girl arrived, making our group slightly bigger. We started moving inside the school, but Anika stayed back.

'What are you waiting for?' Trisha asked.

'I'm waiting for Venki,' Anika replied, her tone as if she were a girlfriend waiting for her soulmate.

My anxiety shot through the roof. What if they're together? What if they're... dating? The thoughts swirled in my head, suffocating me.

A loud engine roar interrupted my thoughts. A bike sped into the school grounds at nearly 100 kmph, skidding to a stop. It was Venkataramana. Though we were not yet of the legal age to ride bikes and all, some of us dared to do so just for fun.

He got off, wearing a formal coat, like a waiter. He pulled out a flower and handed it to Anika.

My feet felt like they were glued to the ground.

We started climbing the school stairs. But then a strange sound echoed through the halls.

I stopped in my tracks.

'What was that?' I whispered to Trisha. 'It sounds... creepy,' she replied.

'Is that a girl?' Anika asked.

'Let's get out of here,' Venkat muttered, already turning back.

But Anika grabbed his hand. 'Let's go in.'

A NEW YEAR

We moved cautiously, passing each room. With each step, Venkat was sweating more. Anika, on the other hand, moved fearlessly.

Then, we reached the science lab. It was locked.

We returned to our classroom. There were six of us. Venkat turned to me. 'Vikram, did you bring the Bluetooth speaker and your phone?'

I was right beside Anika. She could have asked me directly, but she didn't.

Without a word, I pulled the speaker from my bag and placed it on the table, avoiding eye contact with her. She swiftly unlocked my phone and opened YouTube.

But, of course—BSNL SIM. My internet was painfully slow. The video wouldn't even load.

Frustrated, Anika turned to Venkat. 'Give me your phone.'

He immediately grinned, almost too eagerly, and handed it over.

She took the phone and unlocked it—then suddenly, a strange sound blared through the speaker.

A moment of silence. Then realisation struck. It was porn.

The filthy noise echoed in the room. Anika's eyes widened in shock. She glanced at the screen—an open porn site. That idiot hadn't even bothered to close the tabs.

Disgusted, she threw the phone to the ground and backed away from him.

Venkat stammered, trying to explain, but she cut him off with a sharp glare.

'Enough of this shit. I thought you were innocent. All those words you spoke about Vikram—were they fake? You're so selfish!' she shouted, her voice trembling with rage.

She stormed out of the classroom. No one followed her. The room fell into an eerie silence. Then, suddenly—

A blood-curdling scream echoed through the hallway. Anika.

Venkat bolted upstairs like hell itself was chasing him. I followed.

We ran down the dimly lit corridor, reaching the far end where the science lab was located. The door was open.

We stepped inside—

And what I saw stunned me.

A deafening silence filled the air. My head spun in confusion.

Venkat, drenched in sweat, trembled beside me. Then he let out a horrific cry.

'Anika killed a woman! Anika killed a woman!' He turned and ran.

There, in the centre of the room, Anika stood.

Her hands trembled as she held a knife. In front of her lay a lifeless woman.

My heart pounded.

Everyone else fled in terror—except Anika and me. She collapsed, sobbing uncontrollably.

A NEW YEAR

I took slow, cautious steps towards her.

'Vikram, get away from here!' she screamed. 'You'll be involved in this murder case!'

'Anika, calm down. Please. Just breathe,' I whispered.

I knelt beside the woman. My blood ran cold—it was our English teacher.

Her neck had deep scars, her face bruised and burned, some areas marked with cigarette ashes.

Anika cried louder, her body shaking violently.

I examined the teacher's lips, inserting a pencil between them. Teeth marks.

This wasn't just a killing. This was torture.

I placed my hand on Anika's shoulder to comfort her. 'Vikram, don't touch me!' she shrieked, flinching away. 'Anika,' I said softly, reaching for the knife in her trembling hand.

As soon as I took it, reality hit me like a thunderbolt.

Now... I was holding the murder weapon.

'Vikram, have you lost your mind? Do you know what you're doing? Just run! Please... I beg you!'

A sudden noise snapped my attention—the bathroom door creaked open.

A dark figure stepped out.

'Vikram, please go! He's coming!' Anika whispered in terror.

'Who?' I demanded.

'Just listen to me! Please run!'

But I stood firm.

'I'm your friend, Anika. No one can take you away from me.'

I gripped the knife tightly.

The figure stepped forward, revealing himself. A sickening chill ran down my spine.

It was Nagendhar. The school attendant. The same man I bribed for the keys.

He was completely naked.

Anika gasped and shoved me behind a table, trying to shield me from his view.

'Are you ready, Anika?' he spoke, his voice dripping with wicked intent.

'Please… leave me alone, brother. I beg you!' Anika pleaded.

'Just once… just one night. Sleep with me, and I'll spare you.'

Tears streamed down Anika's face. 'Anna, please!'

'Uff,' he sighed, stepping closer. He shut the lab door, sealing us in darkness.

I held my breath. My hands clenched into fists.

He walked towards Anika, his voice sickeningly soft. 'You have such a lovely chest. Why don't you show it to me, baby?'

Anika sobbed harder.

'Why are you crying? You should be grateful! You're getting an opportunity at such a young age. Come on, remove your clothes.'

He reached out and pinched her cheek. 'Remove, baby,' he whispered.

His hand slithered from her neck, creeping towards her chest.

And that was it.

I lunged.

I wrapped an unplugged wire around his neck, yanking it tight. He gasped, his hands clawing at the cord.

He thrashed violently, slamming me against the wall. The impact rattled my skull, and pain exploded through my body.

I gasped for breath.

The monster turned. His furious eyes locked onto me. Nagendhar charged.

His fist connected with my face, sending me crashing to the floor.

Pain shot through my head. My vision blurred. Blood trickled down my forehead.

'Vikram!' Anika screamed.

I reached out weakly, but my body wouldn't move. My limbs were paralysed. My mind raced, but my body was failing me.

I watched in horror as Nagendhar grabbed Anika by the wrist. He threw her to the ground and pinned her down.

'Now, where were we?' he sneered. Anika struggled, kicking and screaming. He laughed.

'Shhh, baby. It'll be over soon,' he whispered, his hands moving to his underwear.

Rage exploded inside me.

With the last ounce of strength in my failing body, I searched the ground. My fingers brushed against something—cold metal.

The knife.

With every bit of force left in me, I hurled it. The blade sliced through the air and struck him. A deep gash appeared on his hand. Blood gushed from the wound.

Nagendhar roared in agony, clutching his bleeding hand. And in that moment—Anika's eyes met mine.

This nightmare wasn't over yet.

He got up, picked up an iron rod and, with a demonic look, charged at me like a bull. He struck my head. I blacked out instantly, blood pouring from the wound like a river.

He turned back to Anika. This time, he pulled down his underwear and reached out, trying to grope her.

I was suddenly pulled into the sky. I saw the sky everywhere. I was running, shouting for Anika, but I couldn't find her.

Then, suddenly, a peacock appeared in the clouds. Its eyes were sharp as it swiftly ran towards me. I covered my face with my hands and closed my eyes. I heard a flute sound. I opened my eyes and was stunned by the appearance before me.

His eyes were sharp, his body shone like a diamond, and he smiled. *It was Krishna, the Lord.*

'What are you worrying about, Vikram?' he asked.

I cleared my throat and answered, 'Anika is in danger, and I wasn't able to help her.'

'Well, what's stopping you, Vikram?'

'He's stronger than me. I can't fight him alone,' I replied.

'Do you know what's the strongest thing on earth? It's your mind. You have the right to perform your prescribed duties, but you are not entitled to the fruits of your actions. Trust in me, stay focused, and fight with determination, leaving the outcome to me. Do not let fear or doubt cloud your mind. *Stand up and face your challenges with courage and faith in the divine plan.*'

Suddenly, I was falling through the clouds, watching the light rays reaching the earth. I witnessed Arjuna and the Mahabharata in my mind.

I stirred.

He saw me regain consciousness and stopped touching Anika. He grabbed another rod and charged at me, but I quickly reached for an old rod nearby. Blood was still flowing from my head, and my vision blurred. He struck my face again, and blood gushed from my mouth. I didn't hesitate. He hit me again, this time on my shoulder, but I didn't react. I punched him in the stomach with as much force as I could muster. He showed no sign of pain, but started hitting me again.

My body was completely motionless. I raised the rod and defended myself. This time, I hit him on the head, chest, and legs, repeatedly, until he finally collapsed.

Suddenly, the police broke down the door. I saw my father run towards me, hugging me tightly and shaking my head. 'Vikram, Vikram, wake up,' he cried.

In that moment, I wished I could die, wishing I'd never seen my father cry for me. I never thought he could care.

I woke up in the hospital, seeing my mother and sister beside my bed. My hand rested on my head, which was completely bandaged.

A month later...

I entered the school. Everyone appreciated the adventure I'd gone through to save Anika. As I entered the class, Anika came in and, all of a sudden, hugged me. My heart skipped a beat, and I almost fainted.

'Are you okay, Vikram?' she asked. 'Yeah, Anika,' I replied.

As the bell rang, we adjusted ourselves at our desks. The teacher entered and praised me in front of the class. Everyone was happy, except for Venkataramana. His anger towards me had grown. He was still aggressive, but I didn't react, nor did I try to talk to him.

Days passed, and Anika stopped talking to the boys, including me.

As the final exams approached, Venkataramana tried hard to talk to Anika. I thought he might try to spread rumours again, but this time, if he said anything about me, she would kick him with her slippers.

After much lying and trying, Anika finally accepted him as a friend. They became friends again, just like before.

The final exams ended. We went to school to receive our progress reports. Anika scored top marks this time, while I was somewhere below—something that had never happened before.

Anika sat alone, and I went to her. My heart raced as I prepared to propose. I was anxious about the outcome. If she rejected me, I'd lose all my self-respect.

I sat next to her. Her sharp eyes met mine. I didn't have the guts to speak. I felt like I might never see her again, so I took a deep breath.

'Anika, I wanted to tell you something.'

'What, Vikram? Why is your face covered with sweat? Haven't you brought a napkin?'

'It's okay, Anika. I have to tell you something.'

'Yeah, speak out.'

My words stuck in my throat. I wanted to tell her I loved her, but couldn't utter a word. I tried, forcing the words.

'What, Vikram? Why are you so anxious? Speak clearly.'

'I think...' I stopped. I couldn't say anything more. 'What?'

'Nothing?' I said and turned other side.

'Just say it, Vikram!'

'I want to play a chess game with you.' 'Now?'

'Let's play,' she said, and pulled out the chessboard from the shelf beside her.

Suddenly, Venkataramana arrived and ran towards Anika. 'Anika, I'll show you something, come on,' he held her hand and took her out of the classroom.

''The grades are too low. We have to change school,' my father spoke while having dinner.

'Yeah, Dad,' I muttered.

Life has a way of making things more complicated than they already are. I've been trying to forget her, though sometimes the thought crosses my mind that I should wait for her, maybe a few years from now. For now, focusing on my studies feels like the best way to escape the pain and keep my mind occupied.

FIVE

CHANGING SCHOOLS

~

On my first day at the school, I entered and saw everyone playing on the ground since it was 9 in the morning. As soon as a swift car entered the gate, everyone rushed towards the stage and stood in lines.

The climate at the school was quite different—it was sunnier than I expected, perhaps because it was situated on top of a hill.

I entered the class and sat on the bench, choosing to sit at the back. The class teacher entered, and the atmosphere was unlike anything I'd seen in my previous schools. The students who sat at the back were playing games, while the girls were watching YouTube videos.

Months passed, and my grades started to drop, spiralling like a stock market crash. I lost interest in studies, even novels didn't excite me, and my motivation vanished. I found myself crossing by the school, seeing Anika twice in six months. No matter how hard I tried to move on, nothing worked out.

Every single day, I struggled—going to school, coming home, and aimlessly surfing the internet on my phone. I sat alone in my room, with thoughts of Anika constantly haunting my mind. I wanted to rid myself of these thoughts, but every time I tried, pain shot through my heart, pulling me back. Even though there were beautiful girls in my class, one thought stayed with me

Anika was perfect.
Perfect like clouds drifting through the sky,
Perfect like the moon that lights the Earth at night,
Perfect like a river flowing through the land,
Perfect like Mount Everest—deadly until you reach the
summit and witness its beauty.

I started writing short scripts during my lonely time. One day, I discovered a channel called MVS (My Village Show), where they featured an old lady, Gangavva, in a comedic role. Inspired, somehow, I managed to arrange the necessary equipment and started shooting short films. Although I was making short films, I didn't have the perfect mobile to shoot videos, edit them, or upload them. I crafted every script on my own. Initially, I received negative comments, but later, everyone appreciated my work. My short films were selected in TFI, and I gained recognition, even without any revenue.

I lost her, but in the process, I found myself. Apart from my academics, I was excelling in everything else.

One night, I came home with a cricket bat. My father, who was sitting at the entrance, watched me with a triggered expression. I noticed he was holding my progress report—it was a border pass.

'What is this?!' my dad asked with immense anger. 'It's my marks, Dad,' I replied.

He suddenly jumped up from his chair, almost slapped me, but stopped just an inch away from my face. He grabbed my bat and threw it away. Like every Indian father, he wanted me to study hard, get into IIT, and then take the UPSC exams.

They never ask about our passions; they are fixed on their own decisions. But I've always been fine with it. My passion is constant; I'll do anything, anything for my father, any job that makes him happy. Because he's the best.

A lot of people talk about my father—his achievements in his department, his kind nature. His kindness is reflected in our family. Literally, everyone in my family has his picture at their home. They respect him a lot—from my mother's side to my father's colleagues to even unknown people—everyone praises his kindness.

As the days of summer passed, I kept myself busy with films and scripts scattered all over my room. Slowly, my mind started to accept that love was not meant for me.

One night, I was peacefully sleeping in my bed when I suddenly dreamt of her. She was laughing at me and gave me a rose. But just as I was about to reach for it, my 5 a.m. alarm rang, waking me up from the dream.

The angel, Anika, kept hitting my mind every day, every hour.

I kissed my mom goodbye.

'Stay safe, Vikram. We'll return before evening,' my mom said as she sat in the car with my father and sister. 'Why don't you join us for your cousin's wedding?'

my father asked. I didn't reply. He knew what was inside me—I hated attending public gatherings.

He rolled up the windows and drove away, and I waved bye to my mom.

'Stay safe, Vikram,' she called out.

At 1 a.m., hunger gnawed at my stomach, forcing me out of bed. The house was eerily silent, with just the distant hum of the refrigerator breaking the stillness. I walked to the kitchen, my bare feet brushing against the cold tiles. Reaching for a plate from the cabinet, I served myself a portion of rice that my mom had prepared before leaving for my cousin's wedding in the morning.

With a sluggish sigh, I carried my plate to the living room, plopped onto the sofa, and turned on the TV. The bright screen flickered in the darkness, casting a dull glow on the walls. I flipped 10 through the channels mindlessly, not really watching anything, until something caught my eye—a red news ticker scrolling across the screen.

I leaned forward, my breath hitching. The words felt like ice against my skin.

CHANGING SCHOOLS

'Swift Dzire hit a lorry while carrying passengers. One person is battling for life in an ICU, while two women have minor injuries. Car No. TS19XXXX.'

The plate slipped from my hands, rice scattering onto the floor. My body froze, a cold wave of dread washing over me. Our car.

For a moment, my mind refused to process the information. My heartbeat pounded in my ears, eyes refusing to accept what it read on the news ticker. My hands trembled as I reached for my pocket—no phone. My chest tightened, panic clawing at my throat. I had no way to call them, no way to know if they were okay.

A helpless sob escaped my lips.

I pressed my palms against my face, trying to steady my breathing, but the weight of fear was suffocating.

A thousand thoughts swirled in my head—who was in the ICU? How bad was it? Were they conscious?

I clenched my fists, my nails digging into my skin as if pain could anchor me to reality. But nothing worked. I was trapped in a nightmare, wide awake, helpless, and alone.

And so, I did the only thing I could. I cried.

I grabbed my bag, packed a few belongings, and headed towards Karimnagar, where my father had been admitted. I reached Karimnagar by bus and didn't take a minute to get off; I started running towards the hospital. The guards saw me running and tried to stop me, but I pushed past them.

I saw my mom, my sister, and a few relatives standing before the ICU. I ran towards them and cried. I never had a strong bond with my parents, as they never kept me close. They usually let me stay in my room most of the time.

I hugged my mom, and she cried too. My uncle came over and tried to calm us down.

'Nothing has happened,' he said. 'He just lost some blood and has a few injuries. The doctors said everything will be fine, and he will definitely return home. Just don't cry, Vikram.'

I stopped crying and walked towards the ICU. The room was filled with patients—some on the brink of death, others gasping for their last breath. I saw my father, bandaged from his legs to his arms and head.

My tears wouldn't stop flowing. I didn't sob; I just took a long breath and walked closer to him.

He sensed me coming and opened his eyes. 'I'm fine, Chinna. Don't cry. It's just life. You have to be strong, be a fighter. *Nanna won't always be with you.*'

I suddenly broke down in front of him. My chest tightened, my throat burned, but the tears kept flowing. I couldn't hold them back anymore.

Stepping out of the ICU, I struggled to contain my emotions. The hospital hallway felt endless, the walls closing in as I tried to steady my breath. The faint beeping of monitors, the muffled whispers of nurses, and the distant cries of other patients filled the air, but I barely registered any of it.

I stayed at the hospital through the night, my body exhausted, my mind in turmoil. At 2 a.m., I found myself back inside the ICU. Without thinking, I lowered myself to the cold floor beside my father's bed. I curled up there, listening to the rhythmic hum of machines, my eyes heavy with exhaustion but refusing to close. Tears streamed down my face, unstoppable, as if my grief had taken on a life of its own.

I don't remember when I fell asleep.

The cries around me woke me up. Loud. Heart-wrenching.

I rubbed my swollen eyes and turned towards the sound. My mother was sobbing, her hands trembling as they rested on my father's lifeless chest. My sister was crying too, her entire body shaking, her face buried in her hands. The weight of sorrow filled the room, suffocating and inescapable.

And then, I looked at my father. Still. Pale. Motionless.

Something inside me shattered, but I didn't cry. I didn't move. I didn't make a sound.

The hospital staff began preparing his body. I watched in silence as they placed him in an ambulance, wrapping him carefully, as if he were still fragile, as if he would wake up if they were too rough. My sister and I sat inside, neither of us speaking. She sniffled, wiping her face with the back of her hand, but I just stared ahead.

My father's body was right there, yet it felt unreal.

She tried to shake me, to get a reaction, but I didn't respond. My gaze remained fixed on his lifeless form.

The journey to our village felt endless. I sat like a statue, unmoving, unfeeling. My body was there, but my mind was lost in the emptiness.

When we finally arrived, I heard the commotion outside, voices rising, people gathering. The moment they took my father's body down from the ambulance, my vision blurred. Everything around me seemed distant, as if I were trapped in a haze.

Hands reached for me, shaking me, calling my name. My relatives, their faces etched with sorrow, tried to pull me back to reality. But I couldn't move. I was frozen, my body refusing to respond.

The loud sobs of the people around me echoed in my ears, yet I felt nothing.

They fell on me, weeping, clinging to my arms, my shoulders. But I remained still, expressionless, unable to react.

Then, the rituals began.

A few people approached my father's body, preparing him for the final journey. Others turned to me, their hands reaching for my clothes. Without protest, I let them remove my shirt. A wooden stick was placed around my neck, a symbolic weight pressing down on me, heavier than anything I had ever carried.

CHANGING SCHOOLS

They bathed my father's body, cleansing him for the farewell. He was then placed on a bamboo stretcher, his form now stiller than ever before.

Someone handed me a pot filled with burning firewood, the smoke rising in soft curls. My hands trembled as I held it. Around me, a few individuals started dancing to the rhythm of drums—a ritual of mourning and departure.

The beats grew louder, echoing in my hollow chest. And yet, I remained silent.

The darkness seeped into every corner of my life. It wasn't like the usual bad days—the kind where you feel low for a while and then bounce back. No, this was different. It was heavier, suffocating, and endless. Every morning felt like a battle, dragging myself out of bed, my body moving but my mind numb.

I started going to school again, at least physically. I walked the same route, passed the same gates, and entered the same classroom. But nothing felt the same anymore. The world around me moved forward, yet I remained stuck, frozen in the past.

I would sit in my usual spot, surrounded by my classmates—people I once joked with, whispered secrets to during lectures—but now, their voices faded into distant echoes. The teacher's words bounced off the walls, but they never reached me. I stared blankly at the blackboard, the scribbled notes a blur, not because I didn't understand them, but because I wasn't really there.

My mind was a storm—thoughts swirling, memories of my father flashing like broken scenes from a movie. His smile, his voice, the way he used to call my name—it all played on repeat, louder than anything the teacher was saying.

I stopped participating in class. When someone asked me a question, I gave half-hearted answers or simply shrugged. My friends noticed—I could tell by the way they exchanged worried glances or hesitated before speaking to me. But no one knew what to say, and I wasn't offering any explanation.

Even when I was surrounded by people, I felt alone. The room could be filled with chatter, laughter, and the clatter of pens and books, but inside, there was only silence. I wasn't really with anyone—not with my classmates,

not with my friends, not even with myself.

The days flowed away, just like stars dimming their brightness.

SIX

FILTERING CONTACTS

~

Anika's birthday was approaching, and I thought of wishing her. She must have an Instagram account, I thought, so I started searching for her by different names—her first name, her surname, her father's name.

I went through 100s of accounts, but I couldn't find her ID.

One night, at 2 a.m., I suddenly woke up, haunted by her thoughts. I felt like I was just an inch away, almost touching her.

I decided to try my luck through our female classmates. First, I searched for Pranathi and sent her a request. I sent several requests from different accounts and then went to sleep.

In the morning, I woke up to find that Pranathi had accepted my request. I stalked through her account but still couldn't find Anika's ID.

For the next three months, I spent six hours a day on Instagram, searching for her account. But I couldn't find it, nor any link that would lead me to her.

The days were getting harder. I was obsessively spying on every Anika account I could find online. I followed 97 different Anika accounts and 56 other female accounts, hoping to find her.

Negative thoughts hit my brain every time, *what if I never get a chance to speak with her? Maybe she wasn't on the phone anymore. Or maybe she was gone forever?*

A Couple of Years Later

The 10th board exams started, and I didn't prepare as much as I should have. I spent most of my time surfing the internet, still trying to find her contact information. One day, I finally decided to try reaching out to Venkat.

I took Venkat's number and dialled it. 'Hello, Venkat!'

'Hello, Vikram. How are you?' He asked.

I tried to speak in a normal tone so he wouldn't sense my feelings for Anika.

'I'm fine. How are you?'

'How's Anika?' I asked, hoping for any clue.

'I don't know. I've lost contact with her,' Venkat replied. 'Really?' I said, surprised.

'Yeah,' he confirmed.

'I can't believe this, Venkat. You were so close to her,' I said, trying to hold back my emotions.

'Yeah, I had her contact,' he said. 'What's the matter?'

I decided that opening up to him might be the best option. 'I've been in love with her for years, and I want to let

her know.'

Venkat knew that very well, since he had also been in love with her.

'She never loved you,' he said bluntly.

I already knew that, but hearing it from him hurt.

'I know that perfectly well,' I said quietly. 'But are you still in love with her?'

'Yeah,' Venkat replied.

The words stuck in my throat. 'Can I get her number?' I asked. 'No, I don't have it,' he said.

'But you just mentioned that you had her number, Venkat,' I said, frustrated.

'No, I don't have it.'

I was filled with intense anger, wishing I could hurt him for just a minute.

As the days passed, my hunt for Anika didn't show any progress.

The 10th results were announced, and I didn't score well enough. Meanwhile, I saw a poster stating that Anika had come first in her school.

Several More Years Went By

I woke up and was brushing my teeth in the washroom while scrolling through my phone. I checked Venkat's status. It was his birthday, and he had added screenshots of contacts of the people who had put his picture with a caption wishing him a happy birthday.

It was just like a train with more than thirty statuses. I skipped through one by one, and froze at the screen.

Anika's name was on one of them. She had put his picture in her status with the caption: 'Happy birthday, my best friend Venkat. Wishing you the happiest years ahead.'

I threw my phone into the wash basin.

My body collapsed, and I lost consciousness. I didn't know what had happened to me.

It felt like a nightmare. Part of me wanted to ask Venkat for her number right away, but another part of me knew I couldn't. I couldn't bring myself to reply to his status or tell Anika what I truly felt.

Venkat knew I had seen his post, because after that, he kept putting up statuses with love songs, tagging them with the letter 'A' and a heart emoji.

Each status felt like a knife twisting deeper into my chest, leaving me more broken than before.

One day, I texted him again. 'Venkat.'

'Yeah, Vikram?'

'I need Anika's number.' 'I don't have it.'

'Please, Venkat, I need to text her just one message.' 'I told you, I don't have her number.'

My anger flared up instantly. I wanted to hurt him badly, but somehow, I managed to hold my nerves.

'Venkat, I beg you, please.' He sent a laughing symbol. 'Venkat, please... understand.'

He sent another laughing symbol.

This time, I didn't reply. In that moment, it felt like I had lost all my pride, reduced to pleading with someone who only mocked my pain.

Finally, I gathered my courage, took my scooty and headed towards her home, desperate for some sign, anything that could help me find the words to confess how deeply I felt for her—or perhaps just to face the truth.

When I reached her house, I saw a truck parked outside, loaded with household goods. Her father was leaving after locking the gate, his face unreadable. My heart sank. They were leaving. I wanted to rush forward, ask him where they were going, plead for their new address, but my feet felt frozen. The weight of grief from losing my father, the emotional exhaustion, and the overwhelming sense of helplessness kept me rooted in place. I could barely watch them drive away, a part of me dying inside as I realised I had missed my chance to even say goodbye.

The intermediate results were announced, and I was curious, not to check my own results, but hers. I opened my laptop, went to the Indian results portal, and entered her name with her surname, hoping to find a lead.

I wasn't really looking for her marks; I just wanted to find her college code so that I could look for her classmates through the class code mentioned in the hall ticket.

Once I found her college name, I downloaded the entire list of colleges in the state and carefully searched through it. That's when I found that she had moved to Karimnagar.

Excited, I immediately searched for her college on Google and Instagram, hoping I could trace her through an official page or a student group. But found nothing, no luck. So, I took her hall ticket number. This time, instead of typing it correctly, I randomly typed the last two numbers from her hall ticket and a few others that seemed similar from her college.

I wrote their names in the book and searched every single name. I found a few people on Instagram and followed some of them.

In the middle of all this, I got a call from Shushank— my old school friend and partner-in-crime when it came to Anika. He used to update me on everything about her.

He was the one I had forced to get her number, but she never gave it. At that time, he had managed to get her to scribble it somewhere, but unfortunately, he misplaced the piece of paper on the way back home.

'Hello, Shushank!

'Vikram, I've got the number! She didn't write it on a piece of paper; she actually wrote it in my class notes. While I was selling those old books, I found her number. Here you go. But be careful, it might be a family member's number, not hers.' He sent me the number over WhatsApp. After years of sleepless nights and spying on hundreds of Instagram and Facebook accounts, I found what I thought was her direct number—but it turned out to be her sister's.

More Time Elapsed

Although I had her number, I chose not to text her right away and wait for the right moment—her birthday was next month.

Day by day, my anxiety grew. I certainly wanted to text her many times, but I kept reminding myself to stop.

Finally, it was her birthday.

I typed: Happy birthday, Anika. She replied: Thanks.

That reply hit me so hard. I had been searching for her madly for many years, imagining countless conversations... and all I received was a simple 'thanks.'

I was eager to interact, yet I waited a couple more days before trying again.

'Hey Anika, how are you?' I texted her while heading towards the Xerox centre to get some documents copied.

I got a quick reply: 'Who gave you this number?'

Her cold response caught me off guard. I quickly texted back: 'I'm sorry if I said anything wrong. I'll delete the number. Bye.'

She replied: 'This is my family's number. If anyone sees this, it could cause problems for me.'

I texted back with an apology: 'I'm really sorry.'

The Xerox machine operator handed me a stack of 200 copies. As I struggled to organise them, my phone buzzed again.

'Where are you studying now?' She asked.

Leaving the papers aside, I typed back: 'I can't say that yet. Where were you all these years?'

She replied: 'I'm in Karimnagar, but how do you know my birthday so accurately?'

I decided not to reveal the truth and made up a story. I typed: 'Well, one of your friends posted your birthday status, so I thought of wishing you.'

Before I could hit send, I received another message: 'No one knew it. No one ever wished me.'

I cleared my earlier message and simply wrote: 'I just remembered, Anika.'

'Hmm, just tell me, who gave you my number?' She pressed.

I replied: 'A common friend.'

She demanded: 'Who's that? Just tell the name.'

'I can't. But don't worry, your number is safe with me, okay?'

She finally agreed: 'Okay.'

Just then, my friend, who was waiting for the documents, started calling me frantically.

'Come fast, Vikram.'

I immediately texted Anika: 'I'll delete your number, Anika. Bye.'

She replied: 'Bye!'

I quickly arranged all the papers and rushed to hand them over to my friend.

A Year Went By

On her next birthday, I gathered the courage to message her again.

I texted her: 'Happy birthday.'

A cold reply came: 'Who is this?'

I was stunned and dejected. Despite having my display picture set, she didn't recognise me.

I asked, still hoping: 'Is this Anika?' No, came the reply.

A sad frown spread across my face. Once again, the distance between us felt impossibly wide.

'Who is this?' Another reply came from the other side. 'This is Anika's sister.'

'Name?'

Why are people so interested in names? I thought, but I typed, 'Vikram.'

'Oh, Vikram!'

'Do you know me?'

'Yeah, I saw your short film once.'

'Hmm, Anika doesn't have her personal phone?' 'No, she doesn't. And we don't talk to boys.' 'Bye,' I ended the conversation.

'Who gave you this number?'

'Some of my friends. It's private. Nothing's going to happen. I'll delete the number.'

'Bye,' she ended the conversation.

Two Days Later

I felt so lonely and frustrated. My professional life was a mess. My friends had betrayed me, and nothing felt right.

I had lost myself. My regret for not telling Anika that I loved her was getting worse, fuelling my anxiety.

What if I had proposed to her? Well, she probably would've said no.

Still...let me try. 'Hey, Anika.'

Hours passed. Then came her reply:

'What do you want? Why are you texting me?'

I texted: 'Just give me five minutes, I'll end everything.' She replied: 'What?'

I wrote: 'Anika, I've had a crush on you for 10 long years. I know you probably hate these things, but I had to say it one day.'

Her texts paused for a few seconds, and then she replied.

'Is this a prank?' Frustration boiled over.

'Anika, how should I even prove that my feelings for you are real?'

She asked: 'Is that real?' I replied: 'Yes, Anika!'

She didn't take the time to shoot back: 'I'm sorry, Vikram.'

I didn't need an apology; I wanted my love to be reciprocated. I didn't reply. I kept staring at my phone as tears started flowing uncontrollably. The world around me disappeared for minutes as I collapsed onto my bed. My heart was truly broken this time.

Suddenly, a message popped up: 'Why can't we be friends?'

I didn't reply for minutes. I knew this message could lead to something complicated. Was I entering into a situationship? I didn't think about the consequences and decided to text: 'I need some time. What about tomorrow?'

'Okay, bye,' she replied, ending the conversation.

That thought stayed with me, and I knew I had to do something. I decided to propose in another way. I held my anxiety for two days, then I called one of my female friends to ask how her boyfriend had proposed.

I searched for ways to propose, but nothing clicked. Finally, I texted:

'Anika, I love you so much. I want to be with you through everything—happy or sad, all my life and beyond. Please don't reply right now, just take your time. But please text me within five days.'

After many anxious and annoying hours, came the reply:

'Why can't we just be friends?' 'Okay,' I texted back.

'Bye,' she immediately replied. I didn't text her again.

Every day, in fact, every few minutes, I checked my mobile, hoping to see her message. I received messages, but only irrelevant and unwanted ones.

After a week, I finally texted her: 'Hey, how are you?' It got delivered after an hour. I was holding onto my anxiety, trying to talk to her.

I was dying to see her message, and kept opening WhatsApp frequently. Then, suddenly, there was a beep again. I opened it quickly, but it was yet another irrelevant message.

I was drowning in anxiety.

Then, there was another beep. This time, it was her message.

'Hey,' she'd texted. 'How are you, Anika?'

'Yeah, I'm good.' She didn't even ask about me. 'What are you doing now?' I asked.

'Nothing,' she replied.

Her single-word replies after I had waited so long were messing with my head. Nevertheless, I continued.

'How's everyone in your family?' I asked. Again, one word from her: 'Good.'

I dragged that boring conversation for thirty minutes. Every time I texted her, she'd reply in five minutes, but only with one-word answers.

As usual, I started to overthink the possibilities of being with her.

Her re-entry into my life felt like digging my own grave. Nothing was going right for me. Life wasn't getting better, and my filmmaking career had stalled due to the unexpected turns in the industry.

I was suffocating under anxiety and anger.

Many times, she would shout at me, but I kept quiet, trying to remain positive.

SEVEN

UNEXPECTED REALITY

～

The sounds of laughter hit my ears. I woke up and turned towards the clock. It was 6 a.m. I swiftly rubbed my eyes and glanced around. I went to the wash basin, splashed some water on my face, and stepped outside to follow the noise.

Women were dressed neatly in the colony lane, drawing *muggu* (kolam) on the road in front of the houses. Suddenly, one woman raised her voice, followed by another. Their words escalated, and soon, they were in a heated argument. The entire group of aunties gathered around them, forming a circle.

The two women, frustrated, grabbed each other and started pulling. They fought, and fought, while the others stood around and watched, seemingly enjoying the scene. It felt like a twisted spectacle, and I had no desire to be a part of it. I immediately felt something stirring inside me, so I grabbed my scooty, and sped off from the fight club.

I pushed my scooty to its maximum speed, heading straight towards Anika's house. The road was filled with vehicles, but I didn't stop for a second anywhere.

When I entered her colony, my heart started pumping hard. My anxiety grew as I realised I was about to witness Anika after four long years. My scooty slowed down to a crawl as I entered her lane. The chance to actually see her was slim—only about 1 per cent—since she was living in another town.

I kept looking at every girl's face, but I couldn't find her. I reached the end of the colony, feeling disappointed, and started turning back. Many women stared at me, probably thinking I was some kind of rogue, but I didn't stop to look at any of them. Then, out of nowhere, my eyes locked with a girl's. My heart almost skipped a beat, and my anxiety hit its peak.

It was Anika.

She wore a mask on her face, just like people did during the COVID-19 era. I focused on her eyes for a few seconds. They were like the moon, shining brightly, hiding a million untold stories. She looked at me, her perfectly shaped eyebrows telling tales that I could only guess.

I quickly sped away and returned home.

I collapsed on my bed and switched on my phone. Suddenly, five messages from Anika popped up, and my anxiety shot through the roof. I opened them immediately:

'Why the hell did you come to our colony?'

'Why did you stop near me?' 'You are just a rogue.'

'Don't you have any common sense?'

That's it. I'm bidding you goodbye. Don't text me again. This is the end.

I felt like my body had just fallen onto the bed. I was confused, unsure of what to do next. I quickly texted her back: 'I'm sorry. I didn't mean to watch you. I came for something else and just happened to see you by accident.' I hit the send button, but it didn't show the two ticks.

I opened her profile, but it was empty. I breathed heavily, wondering if she had blocked me.

I waited an entire day, but the message still wasn't delivered. So, I borrowed a friend's phone and texted her from there: 'Anika, I'm really sorry. I didn't mean to watch you. It's my mistake, and I'm regretting it.'

She replied with a simple 'What?'

'Okay, but I can't be friends with you. Please leave.'

My heart sank. I wrote, hoping against hope: 'I'm sorry, Anika. Please forgive me.'

Her reply shattered me: 'But you are not my friend anymore, so leave. Goodbye.'

She blocked me again. I tried again using a different friend's number.

'Anika, I'm begging you, please forgive me.'

'I can't be friends with you. Please leave.'

'Anika, please!'

'Just let me be. Don't text me from different numbers. Just leave me alone.' She texted and blocked me.

She swiftly unblocked and texted:

'Just take care of your filmmaking career. I know you'll do great things, bigger things. Goodbye now.'

She didn't give me a chance to reply before blocking me again. All these efforts—none of them felt like real efforts anymore.

I cried and cried, but nothing seemed to move forward. Maybe this was just how my life was written. I felt completely lost with thoughts that had been lingering inside of me for years, now hurting more than ever.

I took my scooty and headed towards a hilltop in Jannaram, a place with a weird name called Pakir Gutta. The wind at the top of the hill hit my face, cold and filled with humid dust.

Teardrops carried by the wind were laden with the vivid dreams from across the places. Some from orphans, blindly waiting for a miracle—someone to adopt them, someone to call mom and dad. Others from the physically disabled, crying for their bodies to be fixed, even though they know it won't happen until their next life. Yet, they held on to life with millions of hopes.

I decided to start a new chapter of my life, and booked my tickets for Mumbai to join a film institute. I couldn't focus on anything else but the film techniques that I was about to learn.

As the train screeched to a halt at Chhatrapati Shivaji Maharaj Terminus, the chaotic rhythm of Mumbai greeted me—honking taxis, hurried footsteps, the distant cries of chai vendors. I stepped onto the platform, my backpack slung over one shoulder, my heart heavy with the weight of both ambition and loss.

The city smelled of rain-soaked concrete and restless ambition. The air was thick, not just with humidity, but with the unspoken stories of a million dreamers who had arrived before me, each chasing something bigger than themselves. I was one of them now.

My phone buzzed—a reminder of everything I had left behind in Jannaram. The streets back home felt quieter in my mind now, distant, almost unreal. I had carried my heartbreak with me, tucked between the pages of an unwritten script, buried under the weight of silent memories. She was nowhere near me, yet everywhere. In the love songs playing on a taxi's radio, in the scent of the rain-soaked wind, in the faces of strangers passing by.

But Mumbai didn't care. It moved forward, indifferent to my past, offering only two choices: drown in what I had lost or chase what I had come for.

I adjusted my backpack, took a deep breath, and stepped into the madness.

The platform was full of life, eagerness, and purpose, and I could feel that wave of energy. The scent of steaming vada pav mixed with the metallic tang of train tracks. Hawkers shouted in Marathi, selling everything from cutting chai to pirated novels. The ceiling was high, grand, covered in intricate carvings, and the stained-glass windows caught the morning light like something out of a historical epic.

My bag felt heavier, not just with luggage but with the weight of change. I had finally arrived in Mumbai.

Outside the station, the air was thick with humidity and ambition. Taxis, rickshaws, and BEST buses moved like synchronised chaos. The sound of life—honks, chatter, the occasional street musician—created a rhythm only Mumbai could produce. I hailed a Kaali-Peeli taxi and got into it. I noticed the driver barely making eye contact before accelerating into the madness of the city.

Skyscrapers rose above crumbling chawls. Massive billboards of Bollywood stars flashed by, whispering dreams to those who dared chase them. I saw a film poster and smirked—one day, maybe, my name would be up there too.

The roads twisted and turned, leading me deeper into the city's belly. Past Marine Drive, where the sea stretched endlessly, past the red buses packed with office- goers, Mumbai was not just a city; it was a living, breathing script, waiting to be filmed.

As we neared my destination, the realisation settled in—this wasn't just another trip. This was the beginning of something bigger. A story I was about to write, not just in words, but in frames and reels.

The filmmaking school wasn't just a place—it was a different universe altogether. The moment I stepped inside, the air smelled of fresh coffee, old books, and something intangible yet powerful—dreams in the making. The walls were lined with posters of cinematic legends—Scorsese,

Hitchcock, Ray, and Guru Dutt—watching over every aspiring filmmaker who walked these halls.

I was no longer just an observer of stories. I was here to create them.

The first few days were a whirlwind. Our mentor, a seasoned filmmaker with silver hair and sharp eyes, stood before us and asked just one question:

"What is cinema to you?"

Some answered with technical jargon—frame rates, aspect ratios, mise-en-scène. Others spoke about emotions, how films made them feel something they couldn't express in words. I stayed silent, absorbing every answer, knowing that somewhere between craft and emotion lay the true essence of filmmaking.

We learned how a single blank page could transform into a universe. Words weren't just words; they were cinematic moments waiting to be captured. Every scene needed an arc, every character a purpose.

The way light falls on a subject changes everything. We held cameras, adjusted angles, and learned how shadows could tell stories as much as the actors. The first time I held a professional camera, I felt like I was touching power itself.

'A film is made in the edit room,' they said. Cutting, pacing, blending emotions—it felt like playing with time itself. A second too long could kill a scene. A second too short could steal its impact.

I never realised how silence could be louder than noise. How a single heartbeat sound effect could change an entire moment.

It was overwhelming, intoxicating, and exactly what I had been searching for.

Everyone here carried stories in their eyes. Some were born into the industry, their confidence unshaken. Others, like me, came from nowhere, armed with nothing but passion.

There was Rohan, the guy obsessed with sci-fi, always talking about how he'd be the next Nolan. Meera, a quiet but fierce girl whose short films left you staring at the screen long after they ended. Zaid, the editor who could turn chaos into poetry with a few cuts.

And then, there was Arohi.

The first time I noticed Arohi, she was arguing with our mentor over a scene in a classic film. She had strong opinions, unfiltered thoughts, and the kind of confidence that made you want to listen.

'Cinema is supposed to be raw,' she said, crossing her arms. 'If it's too perfect, it's lifeless.'

I didn't know why, but I smiled. I liked the way she thought.

At first, our interactions were brief—a passing comment about a scene, a shared coffee during a break. But something about our conversations felt natural, unforced.

One evening, as we stayed back after class to work on an assignment, she casually asked, 'Why are you here?'

I hesitated before answering. 'To tell a story no one else can.'

She studied me for a moment before nodding. 'Good.'
'That's the only reason worth being here.'

From that moment, Arohi became my closest friend. We brainstormed scripts together, debated over films till late at night, and pushed each other to do better. She wasn't just a classmate—she was the first person in this city who truly understood what drove me.

As days turned into weeks, I realised something: filmmaking wasn't just about learning techniques or handling a camera. It was about seeing life differently. About finding beauty in the ordinary. About knowing that every person, every silence, every fleeting glance had a story waiting to be told.

Between coffee breaks and late-night script discussions, something unspoken grew between us. We weren't just classmates; we were a crew, a cast, a story in motion. Each of us played a role—Rohan, the dreamer; Meera, the perfectionist; Zaid, the silent genius; Arohi, the rebel. And me? I was the observer, the one soaking it all in, stitching moments into memories.

One evening, as we sat on the steps outside the campus, exhausted from a long day of shooting, Arohi leaned back and sighed.

'You know who we remind me of?' she said, staring at the distant skyline.

Rohan smirked. 'Don't say some indie film reference.

We won't get it.'

She rolled her eyes. 'No, idiot. We're like a prequel to something big. Like a film before it becomes a blockbuster.'

I grinned. 'Like Shah Rukh Khan before he became *King Khan*?'

A hush fell over the group. Not because it was an odd reference, but because it was the perfect one.

We all knew the story—a boy from Delhi with no connections, no godfather, no silver spoon. Just raw ambition and an unshakeable belief in his dreams. He came to Mumbai like we did, wide-eyed and relentless, standing outside film studios with nothing but talent and a hunger to prove himself.

He wasn't the strongest, the tallest, or the conventional hero. But he had something better—an undying spirit. He turned rejection into fuel, struggles into stepping stones, and in time, the world bowed to his name.

From sleeping on benches to owning Mannat. From small TV roles to conquering Bollywood.

Shah Rukh Khan didn't just become a star—he became an emotion, a legacy, a belief that anyone, from anywhere, could rewrite their destiny.

Arohi smirked at me. 'That's the energy we need.' Meera nodded. 'So what do we call ourselves? The next SRKs?'

I chuckled. 'Nah. We're something else. Something new.'

And in that moment, beneath the flickering streetlight, under the vast Mumbai sky, we weren't just students anymore. We were future filmmakers, ready to take on the world.

The day we graduated, my friends celebrated like it was the end of a movie—one with a perfect, happy ending. They packed their bags, booked their flights, and set off on a world trip, chasing sunsets in Santorini and sipping coffee in Parisian cafés. Their social media was flooded with pictures—arms stretched wide at the Eiffel Tower, feet buried in the white sands of Bali.

Me? I didn't have that luxury. I had a different journey ahead.

While they roamed the world, I roamed the streets of Mumbai, script in hand, knocking on doors that refused to open. Office to office. Meeting to meeting. Rejection to rejection.

Harsh Reality

I met directors—some well-known, some barely starting out. I sat in plush offices where assistants barely looked up from their phones. 'Leave your script. We'll get back to you,' they'd say, sliding it aside, already forgetting my name.

Some were polite, some brutally honest. 'This script lacks soul.'

'It's good, but not good enough.' 'You're too new. Get experience first.'

Every rejection felt like a slow punch to the gut. Each one chipped away at my confidence, but I told myself— Shah Rukh Khan must have faced this too. Every legend has.

Mumbai has a way of testing you. It gives you dreams and then watches silently as you struggle to prove you deserve them. The same streets where dreams are born are also where they die.

I spent days waiting outside production houses, hoping for a five-minute pitch meeting that never came. Nights were spent staring at the ceiling of my tiny rented room, script pages scattered around, wondering if I was just another fool chasing an impossible dream.

I could've stopped. I could've packed up and left, just like countless others who came here chasing cinema and left with empty pockets and broken hearts.

But I didn't. Because I wasn't here to try—I was here to make it.

And so, while my friends wandered the world, I wandered the city, still chasing my first 'yes.'

Because one 'yes' was all I needed.

At some point, the weight of rejection became unbearable. The scripts I once poured my soul into now felt like dead weight in my bag. The fire that once kept me going had turned into flickering embers, barely holding on. One evening, after another pointless meeting where a director didn't even bother to read past the first page of my script, I walked aimlessly through Mumbai's crowded streets. The city, once alive with possibilities, now felt suffocating. The neon lights blurred into a haze, the honking of rickshaws mixed with the distant sound of waves crashing at Marine Drive.

That night, I made a decision. I was done.

I booked a train ticket, packed my bags, and left Mumbai without looking back.

As the train rumbled through the night, the city lights fading behind me, my mind wasn't on my failure. It wasn't on the directors who dismissed me or the dreams I had abandoned.

It was on Anika.

Her laughter echoed in my ears—the way she used to tease me, the way she saw through my silence. The countless conversations I had imagined we had. I used to talk to myself about Anika.

I stared out of the window, watching the darkness stretch endlessly. Had she ever thought about me the way I thought about her? Did she even know how much she still haunted me?

Maybe life wasn't about chasing dreams or proving something to the world. Maybe I had been running all along—running from something I couldn't face.

I closed my eyes. Going home felt like an ending. But deep down, I knew it wasn't.

The bus entered Jannaram, blowing its horn. The road through the forest reminded me of a fight scene I had shot here with Sandeep the other day.

I stepped off the bus. My beard had grown so much that no one could recognise me. I hadn't informed my mom about my arrival—I wanted to surprise her with my sudden appearance. As I walked past the neighbourhood, my neighbours—uncles and aunts—gave me strange looks.

They didn't recognise me, as my new appearance was unfamiliar to them. I simply smiled and moved on.

I opened the gate to my house. My mom was sitting there, earphones in, watching a YouTube video. She didn't notice me. I slowly walked closer and suddenly hugged her. Shocked, she gasped and then burst into tears. She slapped me out of love, her anger revealing the pain she had endured during my absence. She lost control and cried loudly.

My mom loves me so much that she can't bear my absence for even a single day. But she had been without me for two years. I held her, trying to comfort her, just as my sister walked out.

A little while later, I opened my eyes to the aroma of delicious food wafting from the kitchen. My mom had prepared a dozen dishes just for me, eager to feed me after all this time. Her love was unconditional.

'Get ready fast! Eat everything!' she said excitedly. 'You made all this, Mom? I love you!' I exclaimed.

'Laxmi aunty helped me,' she replied with a smile.

Kochi 1999

That year the winds of change were more than just a force of nature. They were a reflection of the storm brewing in the hearts of Mohan uncle and Laxmi aunty. The city of Kochi, once filled with the sounds of their shared laughter, now stood silent as their families, bound by tradition, refused to accept the bond they had forged.

Mohan, a man of quiet strength and unwavering discipline, stood tall in his army uniform. The uniform that had been his pride now became the symbol of their separation. Laxmi, graceful yet fierce in her love, stood by him, her eyes reflecting the anguish of the moment.

'Laxmi, they won't understand. We can't stay here anymore,' Mohan uncle's voice broke through the heavy silence. His hands, calloused from years of service, trembled as he reached for her.

Laxmi aunty, her heart torn between the love for her family and the love for Mohan, took a deep breath. The words her father had said still rang in her ears:

'You can't marry him. He's an army man. He'll leave you alone for months, years even. What kind of life is that?' But none of those words mattered now. Love had found its place in their hearts, and no amount of tradition or disapproval could erase it.

With nothing but a small suitcase, Laxmi aunty turned away from her family home, the place that had once been her sanctuary. She didn't look back. Mohan uncle, ever the protector, led the way, his resolve unbroken despite the weight of the rejection that still lingered.

As they walked through the streets of Kochi, the storm outside intensified, as if nature itself was echoing their inner turmoil. The rains fell in sheets, and the winds howled as if to carry them away. But nothing could wash away the love that had rooted itself so deeply between them.

They reached the train station, the platform barely visible through the thick mist. Their destination: Jannaram, a place unknown but filled with promise.

'We'll start over there, Laxmi,' Mohan uncle said, his voice steady despite the turmoil in his heart. 'A new life, just the two of us.'

Laxmi aunty nodded, her fingers gently brushing against his. She had no doubts now. The storm outside mirrored their journey—uncertain and violent—but they would weather it together.

As the train chugged along, slicing through the downpour, Laxmi aunty's thoughts were consumed by what they had left behind. Life in Kochi, the faces of family members who had once been her everything, now distant memories, like the fading echoes of a forgotten song. But beside her, Mohan uncle sat like an anchor, strong and silent, offering her a sense of security in the chaos.

'Mohan,' Laxmi aunty whispered, her voice barely audible over the storm outside, 'Do you think we'll find happiness in Jannaram?'

Mohan uncle squeezed her hand, his gaze unwavering as he replied, 'Happiness isn't found in places, Laxmi. It's found in moments, in us, in this. I'll never let you down.' And in that simple promise, Laxmi aunty found the courage to move forward. They were no longer just escaping their families' expectations—they were embracing a future that they had chosen, together.

I spent a good three days at home, lounging in the comfort of my bed, our sofa and mom's lap, reconnecting with my mom and sister. More than anything, though, I finally got a chance to catch up on sleep, allowing my body and mind to recover from relentless fatigue which had accrued over days and months.

On the fourth day, I planned to visit Laxmi aunty's home in the evening. When I reached there, she was watching TV. As soon as she saw me, she got up with happiness, excitement writ large on her face. I walked up to her and gave her a half-hug.

'Vikram, you've grown so much, man! Good to see you,' she said.

I smiled gently as she ran her hands through my hair. 'Man, why is your hair so long? You look so handsome!' she added.

Aunty is like a second mother to me. She has no sons, only a daughter. Uncle's strict army discipline led them to stop with just one child. Since uncle was often away on duty, aunty was left alone with Mathura, her only daughter.

Mathura, the daughter of Laxmi aunty, is sweet, innocent, and a total book nerd. She was the one who gave me *Half Girlfriend*. Our friendship has always been unique, especially in a society where men and women talking freely is often frowned upon. But unlike the narrow-minded gossipers around us, we've always been very close.

Mathura has been fascinated with photography since childhood. I still remember when uncle brought home a new camera—her excitement was contagious. She used to film everything around her, including me. She cares for me deeply; I'll never forget how, when I had dengue and my parents weren't home, she stayed with me for three days, looking after me.

Our summers were simple but memorable. We used to watch films or series in my room, which had a projector. It became a routine—almost every evening, we'd watch something together. Many times, she'd fall asleep beside me, and when I stayed at their house, I'd sleep next to her. Our bond was that close. Naturally, this closeness sparked rumours, and gossip about us spread far and wide. But thankfully, our parents were always supportive and never doubted us.

As I sat with aunty while she shared some snacks and sweets. 'What do you want to eat today? Chicken?' she asked warmly.

'Aunty, do you know how to make biryani?' I teased. 'No, Nani, I don't,' she replied with a laugh.

114

'Well, I know how to make biryani!' I said with a grin. 'Wow, really? When and where did you learn?' aunty asked, surprised.

'In Mumbai. I had a Hyderabadi friend who taught me,' I replied.

'Alright then, let's make it tonight!'

That evening, we made biryani together. Aunty, my mom, my sister, and everyone loved it so much that they joked I must've worked in a restaurant instead of studying filmmaking!

Later that night, aunty woke me up. 'Vicky, I need my BP tablets. They've run out.'

I quickly got up, splashed water on my face, and rushed to the pharmacy nearby. After handing over the list of medicines to the pharmacist, I wandered around the store, looking for a charcoal face wash. Finally, I found one and was checking its details when someone tapped on my shoulder.

I glanced to my left, and the men at the counter were staring at something behind me. I understood who it might be. Adjusting my goggles, I turned to face her.

'What a surprise! Mathura! When did you get here?' I asked, smiling.

'Just now! Aunty didn't mention you were coming back either,' she replied.

'I wanted to surprise everyone,' she said. "For holidays?" I asked.

'No, I got the news you were here and caught the flight this morning,' she said.

Mathura is pursuing medicine from AIIMS Delhi. Like her mother, she's beautiful. Many people, back in school, teased me to propose to her since she was an icon— someone almost everyone had a crush on. But I never saw her in that way; we just weren't meant to be in that space. Interestingly, she only ever talked to me, ignoring other boys entirely.

'You should've called me, Mathu, to tell me you were coming back,' I said.

'Yeah, yeah! As if calling you makes any difference. Have you even seen your phone in the last two years? I've dialled your number hundreds of times with no response!'

I sighed. 'I stopped answering calls after Anika left. I just wanted to leave everything behind.'

Her tone softened. 'I'm sorry. I didn't know. But still, you could've at least texted me.'

'I used to be busy…'

'Busy with what or whom?' she teased.

We left the pharmacy and headed home. Suddenly, my heart started racing. Anxiety hit me hard as a scooty sped towards us. It almost collided with us.

'*Kya hua?*' Mathura asked, concerned.

'Nothing,' I replied, shaking it off. But my eyes caught something or someone. A girl with long hair, her ribbon untied, strands falling onto her shoulders as she spoke on the phone. My chest tightened. Was it Anika?

No. It couldn't be. But these glimpses of her had been haunting me ever since Mumbai.

We reached home, and I handed the tablets to aunty. Then, I called Sandeep. 'Hello, where are you?'

'At home. Who's this?' He didn't recognise me because I've dialled through my new number.

'It's Vikram.'

'Hey, where have you been all these days? How's filmmaking going?'

'It's good!' I said, laughing.

Sandeep rushed over to my house. Meeting an old friend after so long felt like therapy. We laughed, reminisced about the jokes, the fun, the parties, even the awkward moment when we watched our first adult video together. But when the topic of relationships came up, the laughter always carried a trace of pain.

Mathura came to my room all of a sudden at midnight, alone. I was sitting at my table, trying to reconnect the shapes to build a story.

'Vikram, who's she? Are you still continuing with that relationship?' she asked.

'What made you come here in the middle of the night?' I asked, crossing my chair toward Mathura, who had sat on my bed.

'No reason, just like that. I was curious to know,' she said.

'Why so curious about someone else's life?' I countered.

'Someone else? You're my best friend and everything…' she stammered, struggling to find her words.

'Best friend? I'm not anyone's best friend. I am me, myself. I don't belong to anyone.'

She fell silent, her face showing clear signs of being upset.

'That crush from school… she blocked me after we became friends.'

'Does that mean she's never coming back?'

'Why are you so invested in this now?' I asked, puzzled. 'I brought you something,' she said, changing the topic. 'What?'

'I saw your phone this morning—it had a broken screen.'

'So?'

'I brought you this,' she said, handing me a gleaming, brand-new iPhone.

I was shocked and surprised. 'Where did you get all that money?'

'Savings!' she replied with a cheeky smile.

'Why did you do this? Just keep it for yourself.' 'Take it, or I'll share your love story with aunty!'

Reluctantly, I took the phone. If she revealed my love story to Mom, I'd never be forgiven for the rest of my life.

'Let's watch a film!' she suggested.

'Film? Is our projector still working?' I wondered, rising from my chair and checking the projector. I switched on the projector, and it flashed onto the screen, showing it was indeed working.

I opened Netflix and played Animal. We sat on the bed together. This time, she sat closer than usual. It reminded me of our childhood days, but I wondered if she forgot that we were now twenty-one.

As the film's songs played, she rested her head on my shoulder and hugged my arm tightly.

Fourteenth September arrived. It was my birthday. I woke up early in the morning and checked my phone, where I saw many birthday greetings. Slowly, I scrolled through the statuses and came across Mathura's. She had edited almost every video she had ever shot of me since childhood—me batting in cricket, receiving school prizes, flying my drone, and moments of us together as kids, including a clip of us fighting when we were five years old. Everything was beautifully compiled and posted with a touching background song.

Suddenly, there was a knock at my door. I swiftly opened it—it was Mathura.

'I came at midnight, but you didn't open the door,' she said.

'I was sleeping then,' I replied.

'I had a birthday surprise for you.' 'Hmm, leave it. Thank you for the video.'

'Come on, freshen up! We're going to the temple. Hurry up, you lazy, dumb!' she said with a playful scold.

I quickly got ready, dressed in a traditional outfit, and entered the car with Mathura. Together, we headed to the temple.

As we completed four rounds around the temple, we entered the sanctum to stand before the statue of Lord Krishna. We approached the priest, who placed his hands over our heads and blessed us, saying, '*Dirgha Sumangalibhava*,' a blessing typically given to couples.

'No, we're just friends,' I quickly clarified with a nod. As we stepped out of the temple, Mathura became the centre of attention. Her sun-kissed face seemed to glow, capturing the admiration of everyone around.

I went near the car, unlocked it with my keys, and suddenly a wave of current hit my hair—it was something magical, something I had felt when I first met Anika. My anxiety started growing; I could not stop it. I was breathing heavily, and my body felt like it was collapsing.

Mathura entered. 'Hey, are you okay?' 'You're not looking good... Answer me!' she started to panic.

I couldn't answer her. I remained silent as my body lost its strength, and I collapsed.

'What's going on? You're scaring me. Have you taken something? Tell me the truth! Why are you doing this to yourself? You look awful! I don't understand—what's happening to you?!'

She took my arm around her neck and placed me on the seat.

'Stay with me! Don't you dare close your eyes!'

My body was almost motionless, my vision blurry.

'You're hiding something from me, aren't you? I don't know what's going on, but this… this isn't normal. You need help, and I'm not leaving until I know you're okay.'

We reached home, and she directly took me to my room. She gave me warm water and made me lie down on the bed.

I tried clearing my vision by rubbing my fingers over my eyes. I noticed Mathura sitting on a chair with her head resting on the table—she was napping there. I didn't disturb her and quietly left the room to go to the washroom.

By the time I came back, Mathura had started searching the entire room. Her eyes kept darting around, and her hands were rummaging through every corner, turning my room into a complete mess. She eventually found a packet in my bag. Pulling it out, she removed a strip of tablets and examined them closely.

'Alprazolam? Why the hell are you using this?' she asked sharply, her tone filled with concern.

'Simply,' I replied curtly, trying to avoid an argument.

Her expression changed. 'How many milligrams have you taken?' she pressed.

'Twenty,' I muttered, wrapping myself in a blanket and lying down on the bed.

'Why on Earth, Vikram? Are you mad? Stupid? An idiot? Why would you do that? It's seriously harmful! Let's go to the hospital now,' she said in panic. She yanked the blanket off me, grabbed my hand, and urged me to get up. 'Let's move—NOW!'

Her persistence triggered me. 'Just get lost! What are you even doing in my room? Get the hell out of here!' I shouted angrily, loud enough for Laxmi aunty and my mom to come rushing in. They were shocked by my behaviour but didn't say anything. Instead, they took Mathura out of my room.

The next day, Laxmi aunty's temperature spiked so high that we had to admit her to a hospital. I carried a novel along and accompanied her. When we arrived, I saw Mathura. Her eyes were red, and she looked exhausted. I gave her a half-hug to comfort her. 'Don't worry, I'm here. Just take some rest,' I reassured her.

As the hospital was mostly empty, I found an unoccupied bed, sat down, and started reading my novel. Mathura folded her legs and sat beside me, resting her head on my shoulder. She fell asleep, and I noticed how peaceful she looked. She didn't move for hours. Her face told the story—stress from her studies, sadness lingering in her heart, and the anxiety she'd been holding in. She slept like a child, safe and comfortable.

'Vikram, have you eaten anything?' Laxmi aunty asked softly after a long silence. She was lying on the bed, her energy too low to move much.

Mathura woke up, rubbing her eyes with her fingers, then adjusted her glasses. 'Yeah, aunty. How are you feeling now?' I joined in, helping her sit up. Grabbing a coconut from the ground, I peeled the top and handed it to her.

Just then, a woman entered the room with a nurse and took a bed opposite us. Mathura and I decided to move to the verandah outside the room.

The woman struck up a conversation with Laxmi aunty. 'Who are they?' she asked, nodding towards us.

'She's my daughter, and he's…' aunty paused. 'Your son?' the woman asked with interest.

Aunty smiled faintly. 'Yeah, he's like a son to us.' 'Like a son? What do you mean?' The woman's

curiosity deepened.

'He lives next door. We're very close,' aunty explained. 'Are you from Jannaram? Your accent sounds a bit like Malayalam.'

'Yes, I'm a Malayali. We settled here twenty years ago.' 'That's nice. How did you choose this place?'

'It was random, but Jannaram feels like home. It reminds us of Kerala, surrounded by forests.'

'What does your husband do?' 'He's in the army—a General.'

'Okay. So, it's just the two of you here?'

'Yes, but we have them—Vikram, his mother, and his sister. The three of them take care of us a lot. In fact, Vikram is like my own son. He means everything to us.'

The woman thought for a moment and then said, 'Can I say something? Please don't take it the wrong way.

Aunty nodded after a brief pause. 'Go ahead.'

'Well, you see those two?' She gestured towards us. 'They look really good together. Why don't you marry your daughter to him?'

Aunty didn't reply immediately. A smile crept across her face, and her expression became warm. I noticed her looking at us. Mathura was lying comfortably on my shoulder, completely engrossed in watching reels on her phone.

EIGHT

WILL BE FRIENDS AGAIN

~~

As summer arrived, all my friends returned home from their college hostels. It wasn't like before when we used to have two-month breaks. Some came for ten days, others for fifteen. Time hits hard when we look back at the old days—the experiences we went through, the things we created, and the short films we started. They now feel like a daydream. We managed to acquire 100k+ subscribers, making it the top YouTube channel after 'My Village Show'.

We all knew our careers and were sure of what we wanted to be. Everyone dreamed of working in the Telugu film industry. We almost envisioned ourselves working with TFI stars like Prabhas. Shashank dreamed of making a sci-fi film starring him, Varun wanted to cast him as a villain, and I dreamed of ruling the entire industry, just like RGV does.

Those films and Ayn Rand had a significant impact on my thinking and my filmmaking. I started to think rationally, but my past—especially my memories with Anika—kept haunting me. When I try to behave rationally, it tears me up. Her absence drives me crazy. I struggle to make sense of it all.

As time passed, everyone chose different directions, just as typical Indian parents want us to—become job holders. Some cracked the JEE-Advance for the IITs, some joined medicine, but Varun and I remained in this field. Now, Varun has become an influential YouTuber with almost one million subscribers.

Our lives have taken many turns. Our dreams have shattered with our career choices, our egos clashed, yet we remained together—partying, travelling, and having lots of fun. We rode our bikes and scooties through the hills, across the plains, over rivers, and all across Jannaram, exploring the beauty of Kawal Tiger Reserve.

Life, though not always what we want, requires us to adjust to the variations and turns it takes us through. It is like a sea wave. When it hits the sand, it's smooth, but when it crashes against the rocks, it's powerful and massive. Still, we should strive to be like a wave, persistent and adaptable. Just as water flows effortlessly with the current, we too must learn to go with the flow.

The sun was just below the horizon, casting a faint glow across the sky. The ground was cleaned, the bushes were cleared, and the pitch was watered to make it look hard as the ball hit the ground. The wickets were placed, and the entire colony gathered on one side where chairs were neatly arranged, just like before. The entire neighbourhood sat there, eagerly waiting.

The pressure on us was immense. We were the Pragathi Nagar team, facing the Gandhi Nagar team, which had consistently been better than us. We had lost to them many times in the past, and they had just recently won a district tournament.

'Why is this match happening?' I asked Varun.

So, there was some history behind this match. There was a feud between Bhaskar uncle and Ramesh uncle owing to only one car parking slot. Already weighed down by the day's tensions, tempers were flaring. One day, they scrambled to claim the parking spot, leading to a front collision. Bhaskar uncle's bonnet caved in, while Ramesh uncle's windshield was shattered.

Both men stormed out of their cars, their anger spilling over. Heated words flew first, sharp and cutting. In a flash of temper, Ramesh uncle seized Bhaskar uncle's collar. Bhaskar uncle, without hesitation, slapped Ramesh uncle. Within moments, neighbours rushed over to pull them apart, but the damage was done—the clash had drawn battle lines between the two colonies, each refusing to back down.

127

Finally, Ramesh uncle proposed a solution: a cricket match between Gandhi Nagar and Pragathi Nagar. The losing team would have to bow their heads and apologise.

This match was now the talk of the town. The pressure had brought me into the team, specially called to play in this crucial game. Both sides managed to arrange an umpire, a speaker system, and Red Bull cans, dozens of them, to keep everyone energised.

The match began under a blanket of heavy clouds, thick with the promise of rain yet stubbornly holding back. The air was dense, and the ground smelled of freshly watered earth—a reminder of the care taken earlier in the day to make the pitch look hard and fast. The crowd was electric, divided sharply between Gandhi Nagar and Pragathi Nagar. Gandhi Nagar's section roared with confidence, while our side, though smaller, cheered with cautious optimism.

The first over was tense. Sandeep bowled a tight line, but Gandhi Nagar's burly opener with an aggressive stance pushed the ball for a quick single off the very first ball. Bhaskar uncle was keenly watching the match, leaning forward, hands clutching his knees. His face carried the weight of unresolved frustration, his jaw clenched tight as if the match were a personal battle for him. Ramesh uncle, on the other hand, sat with his arms crossed, a smirk playing on his lips as if he were already certain of their victory.

The second over began with Shushank steaming in, his run-up deliberate. The Gandhi Nagar opener, now more confident, lofted the third ball over covers for four.

The ball raced across the lush green outfield, drawing a roar of approval from their crowd. Bhaskar uncle shot a glare towards the Gandhi Nagar supporters, muttering something under his breath. Ramesh uncle, catching the look, chuckled loudly, his amusement echoing even above the cheers.

By the third over, the tension began to rise. Varun was brought into the attack, his slower balls proving tricky. On the fourth delivery, the batsman edged one high towards square leg. I sprinted in, my heart pounding, but the ball slipped through my fingers. The Gandhi Nagar crowd erupted in cheers, and Ramesh uncle jumped to his feet, clapping wildly. Bhaskar uncle stood motionless for a moment, then threw his hands up in frustration, shouting, 'Catches win matches! What are you doing?'

Mathura turned to me from the sidelines. 'Don't let it get to you,' she said firmly, her voice steady but tinged with concern. 'You've got this.'

The clouds hung heavy, the sun barely visible as the match moved into its next phase. The sixth over began with Sandeep returning to the attack, his shoulders squared as he charged in. His first two deliveries were precise, dot balls that drew cheers from our side. Bhaskar uncle's face lit up slightly, his hope reignited. 'That's it, Sandeep! Build the pressure!' he yelled, his voice carrying over the murmuring crowd.

But Gandhi Nagar's captain had other plans. On Sandeep's slower third ball, he stepped out and lofted it cleanly over long-off for a six. The sound of the bat meeting the ball was sharp and unforgiving. Ramesh uncle rose from his chair, clapping thunderously. 'That's how it's done!' he called out, shooting a glance toward Bhaskar uncle.

The Gandhi Nagar crowd exploded, their voices echoing through the ground. On the other side, our supporters were quieter, though a few diehards continued shouting words of encouragement. Mathura, however, sat silently. She wasn't one to panic, but I noticed her biting her lower lip. She leaned towards me during a break between deliveries. 'We need a breakthrough,' she said. 'They're running away with it.'

By the end of the seventh over, Gandhi Nagar had crossed 60, with no wickets lost. The eighth over brought Varun back into the attack. His first two balls were tight, frustrating the batsman, but on the third, a thick edge flew past slip and raced to the boundary. Bhaskar uncle slapped his thigh in frustration. 'Unlucky!' he muttered, shaking his head. Ramesh uncle leaned back in his chair, arms behind his head, clearly enjoying every moment.

The eleventh over brought Prem back into the attack, but Gandhi Nagar's captain wasn't fazed. He flicked the first ball through mid-wicket for a four, a perfectly timed shot that sent their supporters into a frenzy. The next ball, however, brought a chance. The captain mistimed a drive, sending the ball straight towards long-off. Varun positioned himself under it but dropped it at the last moment. The crowd groaned as the batsmen ran two.

Bhaskar uncle threw up his hands in despair. 'These missed catches are going to cost us!' he shouted, his voice thick with frustration. Ramesh uncle, sitting comfortably, couldn't resist. 'Looks like your team doesn't want to win,' he said with a sly grin.

Mathu's expression darkened. 'Focus on the next ball,' she said to me, her tone firm. She was trying to keep everyone's spirits up, but I could see the strain in her eyes. The Gandhi Nagar crowd erupted, their chants growing louder with every run scored. Our side, meanwhile, sat in stunned silence. Bhaskar uncle had his head in his hands, and even Madhu looked shaken. 'We can't afford this rampage,' she muttered under her breath.

The darkened clouds were still hovering, and a cool breeze swept across the ground, as if nature itself was bracing for the climax. Mathu, standing next to me outside the boundary line, turned and said, 'We need something special now. Otherwise, this game will slip away.' We had a target of 130 in fifteen, seemingly a tougher one.

The tension was suffocating. Every ball felt heavier than the last, the weight of expectations pressing down on me. Gandhi Nagar was dominating, their confidence towering over us. But deep inside, something in me refused to give up.

Sandeep went in to bat and hit five fours in four overs, bringing the total to 31/0 at the end of the fourth over. Tensions rose as only 11 overs remained. The crowd stayed silent, showing no excitement. On the first ball of the fifth over, Shushank lofted a shot high in the air—it followed a fielder, and it was the first wicket! The Gandhi Nagar crowd erupted in cheers, while Bhaskar uncle showed no hope in us. Mathura, sitting beside me, remained silent.

Varun and Sandeep took the crease, but the entire fifth over went for dots, with just a single run coming off the last ball, putting Sandeep on strike. A spinner was introduced in the next over. Sandeep stepped out of the crease, attempting a big shot, but unfortunately, he missed, and the ball crashed into the stumps.

Prem was next. He walked in confidently but struggled at first—his first two shots went straight to the fielders. Then, on the next ball, he connected cleanly, sending it soaring for a six! Facing the final delivery of the over, he decided to go on the front foot but got an edge, and the ball went straight into the wicketkeeper's hands. He was out. By the end of the sixth over, we were 38/3.

I took the bat and walked towards the crease while our supporters cheered loudly. Their voices echoed across Gandhi Nagar, silencing their crowd as they focused on the match. I was set to finish the game.

In the next seven overs, I smashed four sixes and six fours, while Varun contributed a few crucial runs from the other end. We reached 118/3 in 13 overs. Our supporters erupted in celebration. Bhaskar uncle, overwhelmed with excitement, took off his shirt and waved it in the air. We needed just 12 runs from the last 12 balls—victory was within our grasp.

Then, the opposition captain took the ball and bowled. The first delivery shattered the stumps. The entire stadium fell into silence. Varun, the sixth batsman, walked in. The next two balls were disastrous—he lost his wicket, followed by another, leaving us at 118/6.

I returned to the crease. The fast bowler charged in, and I struck the ball hard, but it went straight to a fielder, so we ran for a single. Everyone shouted at us not to run because at the other end stood Adharsh, who barely knew how to bat. Rotating the strike was risky. He faced the next ball, missing it by an inch from the stumps. Another delivery—another miss. The tension escalated.

We needed 11 runs from three balls to win, 10 to tie. I didn't push Adharsh to run, but on the next ball, he cautiously placed his bat like a shield, and the ball rolled away, allowing us to steal a single. Ten needed from two balls, 9 to draw. The setting sun cast a golden glow over the field, as the crowd held their breath.

The bowler delivered a yorker—I anticipated it perfectly, stepped forward, and smashed it for a six! The crowd roared.

Now, three runs to tie, four to win. The bowler ran in for the final ball. I swung my bat—the ball soared through the air. The entire crowd watched in anticipation... and then—the crowd roared as the ball went over the boundary—SIX!

We won the match!

The ground erupted. My teammates rushed towards me, shouting, cheering, and lifting me up. I could barely process what had just happened. My chest heaved, my hands shook. I had done it. We had done it.

But then, amidst the chaos, my eyes landed on someone in the crowd.

It was Anika.

She wasn't just there. She was hugging Mathura.

For a moment, everything around me faded. The noise, the cheers, even the thrill of victory—it all blurred. My body felt light, almost detached, as if something deep inside me was unravelling. I had won the match, but at that moment, it felt like I was losing something far more important.

My heart wasn't at ease, nor was it easy to handle. It felt nervous, crumbling inside me. I couldn't describe the pain, nor could I remain silent. My anxiety grew, an unstoppable force within me. I was unable to comprehend my emotions—unable to face the past or steady my breath. The world, which once seemed empty, was now filled with flowers and beautiful moments. I can't label this as happiness, nor can I call it my worst phase. All I can say is this: perhaps God wants us together, yet again.

Later in the evening, as I was standing on my building's terrace, an eagle started circling above me. Its sharp features took me a few moments to recognise—it was indeed an eagle. Suddenly, it dove towards me with an eagerness that I couldn't comprehend. I just stood there, watching, unable to react. It came dangerously close to my head before veering left towards Mathura's terrace.

To my amazement, I saw Mathura and Anika standing on the terrace. Mathura was pointing towards the garden, her finger suddenly shifting to point in the direction of my terrace. Anika turned her gaze and locked eyes with mine. In that instant, my world began to crumble. Time just stopped there. I just collapsed on my terrace.

The last thing I remember was Mathura's voice shouting my name. Then darkness swallowed me whole. When I woke up, I found myself in the hospital. My hand was completely motionless, numbed by the strong glucose that had been injected into it. After two days of being in a haze, I felt strangely refreshed, as if my body had hit the reset button.

The ICU stretched before me, a place of quiet intensity. Machines around me hummed and beeped steadily, their sounds blending into an almost rhythmic pattern. My gaze wandered—the bright white lights overhead were harsh, casting shadows on the smooth, sterile walls. Curtains separated each bed, barely shielding the patients around me, some still as if caught in a battle with time, others weakly moving, their faces pale.

Nurses moved efficiently, their hands adjusting IV lines, checking monitors, and administering care with a practised calm. The faint smell of disinfectant lingered in the air, mingling with the mechanical scent of the equipment.

A doctor walked in, murmuring instructions, their presence commanding yet reassuring.

As I lay there, I felt detached yet oddly present, absorbing every detail. Time didn't feel real—each moment stretched infinitely, yet everything around me moved with a quiet urgency. It was a strange mix of hope and fragility, as if life itself was suspended in the room, fighting to hold on. My eyes fell on the entrance, and my heart started to beat heavily as if I were having another panic attack. Then a nurse ran towards me, accompanied by the sound of the heart monitor. My world shattered suddenly, and I felt uncomfortable. My old memories flashed before my eyes, and I couldn't see anything clearly. My eyelids started to close on their own.

It was Anika, her absence haunted me, her presence almost killed me.

With some difficulty, I opened my eyes and saw Anika and Mathura beside me. Mathura placed her hand on my forehead and comforted me, 'You will be fine.'

'Yeah,' I mumbled, removing the oxygen mask and sitting up on the bed.

I didn't say anything after that. Silence consumed me. 'How are you feeling now, Vikram?' Mathura's voice broke through the quiet, slipping through my ears and straight to my heart, passing through tears I couldn't hold back. I didn't reply. I couldn't control the tears rolling down, nor the emotions tearing me apart from within.

'Do you know Vikram?' Mathura asked Anika. 'Yeah, he was my classmate in school.'

Mathura's expression changed. Her eyes dropped, and in that moment, she realised it—Anika was my Anika. Mathura didn't look well. Her voice faltered as she said, 'Excuse me, I have to go to the washroom.' She sounded off, like something inside her wasn't okay.

I cleared my throat, trying to steady myself, but the tears kept falling. 'Her hug could comfort me,' I thought, 'but her words are only bleeding me.'

Soon, Mathura returned and joined us. She asked with a hesitant smile, 'So, you two were friends before?'

Anika smiled faintly and replied, 'We will be friends again.'

NINE

MY SHADOW KNOWS MY TEARS

~

It was a cold winter night. The bus stand was silent, and the distant barking of dogs echoed faintly in the air. Most tea shops had long since closed, and buses were unloading passengers. In the faint moonlight, I felt cold but strangely relaxed. Anika had come back into my life—the love I had never left. The mental pressure in my head and the pain in my heart seemed to flow away like a quiet stream.

I sat at the bus stand, lost in thought, when Mathura began unzipping her bag. She handed me something, and in the dim light, I couldn't make out what it was. Swiftly, I turned on my mobile torch. It was neatly packed. Carefully, I started tearing off the cover, and to my surprise, it was a watch—my Titan Zoop watch. The same one I had broken back in 2010 while playing. It had been glued back together perfectly, and the time was working fine.

MY SHADOW KNOWS MY TEARS

It was my favourite watch, the first gift my father had given me after I secured the first rank in fifth grade. It wasn't just a watch—it was an emotion, a cherished memory of my father.

'Man, I can't believe this,' I said, my voice trembling. 'You've kept this all these years.'

Mathura smiled faintly. 'Yeah,' she replied. But she didn't seem well—perhaps it was the stress of her hectic MBBS schedule.

This watch was the only tangible memory of my father I had left with, and now it was working again, looking as good as new. As the bus to Hyderabad arrived, Mathura prepared to leave.

She boarded the bus but then suddenly ran back towards me. Her eyes glistened with unshed tears, and her face carried the weight of unspoken words. I didn't ask her what had happened.

She came closer, stood on her toes, and kissed my forehead softly. 'Take care,' she whispered before turning back to the bus.

She didn't wave back. She didn't even look at me from the window as the bus pulled away, leaving me standing there in the cold night, clutching the memory of my father and the bittersweet ache of her departure.

I woke up in the morning to the sound of my doorbell ringing. I rubbed my eyes and headed towards the door. When I opened it, it was Anika. I blinked twice and rubbed my eyes again—was this a dream? This kind of thing had happened thrice in the past four nights.

'What happened?' Anika asked with a smile, staring at me.

This time, it felt real. I had to behave properly. 'Yeah, what's up? Why are you here?'

'I need some curry leaves. I think you have some in your garden. Can you pluck them for me? I couldn't do it myself,' she said.

'Yeah, sure.' I went out, plucked a few branches from the curry leaf plant, and handed them to her.

'Are you free this evening?' Anika asked. 'Yeah? Why?' 'It's my parents' wedding anniversary. Could you help me with some decorations and a surprise? Please?' she pleaded.

'Will do!' I replied.

'Thank you! I'll call you tonight. Please join us,' she said before leaving.

Later in the day, I went to a bakery and ordered a cake in advance. Then I visited a gift shop, picked out a beautiful statue of Krishna and Radha, and got it packed carefully.

That evening, the house was buzzing with excitement. Anika's parents—uncle and aunty—were surprised when they walked into the room. Their faces lit up with astonishment as they took in the decorations. They didn't remember it was their wedding anniversary—perhaps years of life's hustle had blurred such milestones.

Anika, of course, had remembered. She was the one who wanted to celebrate this day for them. Unlike her siblings, who didn't show much interest, she was determined to make it special. She wanted to honour their love and sacrifice, which had shaped her family's life.

We decorated the entire room with strings of fresh marigolds and colourful balloons. The fragrance of the flowers filled the air, mingling with the aroma of the freshly baked cake I had picked up earlier. We placed the small Krishna and Radha statue in the middle of the table—a symbol of eternal love that resonated with uncle and aunty's bond.

I brought a speaker, and we played some of their favourite old Hindi songs—classic Lata Mangeshkar and Kishore Kumar melodies that brought back memories of their youth. Anika had also arranged a slideshow of their old photos on a laptop. As the images flashed across the screen, uncle and aunty's eyes moistened with tears, their smiles growing wider with each picture.

When we called them to cut the cake, the entire colony was there, clapping and cheering. Everyone had come together to celebrate—neighbours, friends, and even the kids from the nearby houses. The room was filled with laughter and warmth, and for a moment, it felt like one big family.

Uncle and aunty cut the cake together, their faces glowing with happiness. Aunty, who was usually reserved, couldn't stop smiling. 'This is the first time anyone has ever done something like this for us,' uncle said, his voice breaking with emotion.

Anika stood beside me, watching her parents. I could see the satisfaction on her face, the pride of knowing she had created a moment they would never forget.

As the night went on, people shared stories, danced to the music, and enjoyed the simple joy of being together. It wasn't just a celebration of a wedding anniversary—it was a celebration of love, family, and the small joys that make life meaningful.

I went up to the terrace to enjoy the cool breeze and the calming moonlight. As I stood there, I heard someone coming up the stairs. Turning around, I saw Anika. Her smile lit up the night, beautifying my heart in ways words couldn't describe.

'Thank you. Without you, this wouldn't have been possible,' Anika said softly.

I smiled but remained silent, unable to find the right words.

'Look at that,' she said, pointing to the sky. A shooting star blazed across the horizon. 'Make a wish—it will definitely come true.'

She closed her eyes briefly and said, 'I wish for Vikram to have the happiest years ahead, along with my family.'

'You don't have any other wishes?' I asked. 'No, I don't. Why do you ask?'

'What about your marriage?'

She smiled lightly. 'My parents will take care of that.'

I smiled again, but this time it was different—filled with emotion. How lucky I could have been if she had accepted my proposal.

'Mathura is lucky,' she said suddenly, her voice soft but certain.

'Why?' I asked, my curiosity piqued. 'To have you,' she replied.

I felt a pang in my chest, unsure of how to respond. 'Nothing like that,' I finally managed to say. 'We fight all the time.'

After a brief pause, I spoke again. 'Hey, are you free tomorrow?'

'Yeah, why?'

'I'm planning a small trip to the forest. Are you interested?'

'Yeah, sure! I'm a travel enthusiast,' she replied.

I took my car out at 4 a.m. and reached Anika's home. By then, she was already ready, tying her shoelaces on the porch.

'So, where are we heading?' she asked.

'Somewhere. Let me keep it a secret,' I said with a smile. On the way, I stopped the car at Indanpally and went into a small shop to buy a jar of coffee. Then, we headed towards Kadem. The roads were surrounded by dense forest on both sides, with a thick layer of fog blanketing everything.

Anika slid open the sunroof and stood up slightly, letting the cool breeze wash over her. Her hair danced with the wind, and her face glowed with happiness. She stretched her arms wide like a bird, embracing the breeze.

'This is so awesome!' she exclaimed, her voice filled with excitement as she adjusted herself back into the seat.

'Yeah,' I said, grinning. 'It'll get even better later.'

She tucked her hair behind her ear with her fingers and cracked the window open a little more, letting the breeze gently flow into the car.

She turned on the stereo, connected via a pen drive, and played Daljit songs. She vibed along, lost in the music. I had reached Kadem and was heading towards Gangapur Road, which was a completely muddy stretch. Since my car was an SUV, I felt safe on those bumpy roads. We had almost crossed 5 kilometres into the dense forest when Anika's face turned pale white; she looked nervous. We reached a point where the vehicle couldn't move an inch further. Outside, it was freezing cold. Suddenly, a pack of dogs appeared—nearly a dozen of them—surrounding us. Anika almost bolted, but I made her stay still. I grabbed a stick and cautiously moved towards the dogs. They backed off and eventually scattered away.

'I'm feeling nervous. Let's head back, please. This is so scary,' Anika pleaded.

'No way. We have to reach there,' I replied firmly.

'Alive?' she asked, her voice trembling.

'Yes, Anika. Just a few more kilometres to go.'

'Kilometres? Man, I can't do it anymore!'

'As long as I'm with you, nothing can harm you.'

MY SHADOW KNOWS MY TEARS

We entered a ghat road and began climbing the hill. The higher we climbed, the harder it became to reach the top. When we looked back, we realised we had already covered about 50 per cent of the climb. The grass bent with the breeze, and the eerie sounds of animals haunted us. At times, Anika would panic, and at other times, she would cling to me, frozen with fear.

Finally, after stumbling and slipping down a few times, we reached the hilltop. It was still cloudy when we arrived. I pulled out a coffee mug I had brought along, and we sat at the edge of the hill. The view was breathtaking—a dense forest stretched endlessly below us, and the hill's sunlit spots peeked through the clouds, creating a magical contrast. I found my destination.

At the summit of the hill, the sunrise point felt like a hidden sanctuary, surrounded by undulating hills and a thick blanket of forest that seemed to stretch endlessly into the horizon. The hill itself was an enchanting blend of flat expanses and gently curving slopes, giving it an almost dreamlike quality. Nestled at the very top stood a weathered watchtower, a sentinel that overlooked the vast, untouched landscape. Right at the edge of the hill, a four-seater chair was placed, offering the perfect vantage point to witness the day's first light. As the sun began to rise, its golden rays painted the sky in hues of pink and orange, gradually spreading across the horizon. The sight was more than just beautiful—it was transformative, as if the landscape itself was coming alive with every passing moment. The peaceful solitude, the cool morning breeze, and the vastness of nature surrounding me made the experience feel surreal. It was far more incredible than I had ever imagined, and in that moment, I felt like I was standing at the very edge of the world, witnessing the birth of a new day.

She sipped from her cup, sitting with her legs crossed, facing my side. Her eyes met mine, and her smile sent shivers down my spine. Up close, she looked diff rent—almost mesmerising. I stared into her eyes for a couple of minutes, lost in the moment. Suddenly, she averted her gaze.

'Hey, look over there—the sunrise,' she said, pointing towards the east.

As the sun began to rise, she grabbed her phone and hurried to capture a timelapse. The golden rays kissed her skin, making it glow, and her beauty left me in awe. I felt alive in that moment. I fell in love with her movements, and I fell in love with her all over again.

I fell in love with her again, maybe not forever,
maybe not ever.
But these moments will heal my heart. Her movements—
The rhythm of my life, my art.

The Following Day

It was 5 a.m. when I got a call from Anika. Her car had broken down, and we needed to go to Karimnagar, which was 100 kilometres away. I took my car and picked her up on the way.

'Vikram,' she spoke in the middle of the journey. 'Yeah?' I said in a comforting tone.

'I'm really sorry... for blocking that time.' 'It's fine,' I said and shifted gears.

'Mathura always used to talk about you. Every word of hers was about you. I never thought I'd meet you again.'

I glanced at her and smiled.

'Mathura is so good. She's my closest friend now. She's such a hardworking person.'

'Yeah, she is,' I replied.

She looked at me and said, 'You're also very sweet. She's lucky to have you.'

'And now, you too.' I smiled.

As we reached Karimnagar, I dropped Anika at the passport office and waited for hours. Feeling bored, I played Eminem – Superman and started vibing to it.

After some time, Anika tapped on the car window. I unlocked the door.

'Yoo! Eminem, still?' Anika asked as she sat inside. 'Yeah, my favourite. I love the wave in his music.'

'I know he's your favourite.' She smiled. 'How?' I asked.

'In school! You don't remember?' 'No... Did I say he's my favourite?'

'No, leave it,' she laughed. 'Man... speak up, please.'

'One day, while you were listening to Superman, I thought you were watching porn. She started laughing but quickly stopped. 'Well, Venkat said that.'

'Really?' I chuckled. 'Well, let's go to a restaurant.'
'Yeah, please! I'm suffocating with hunger.'

We were heading towards Penguin Restaurant when suddenly a guy dashed into our car with his scooty. He came from the wrong side and dashed into us.

The guy fell along with his scooty, and Anika rushed towards him, helping him stand as a crowd gathered.

Suddenly, my heart started to race, my anxiety grew, and my mind went blank. I stood there in shock, my eyes fixed on the scene before me. It was neither what I had imagined nor expected. The guy was Venkataramana—my classmate, Anika's best friend.

We reached Penguin Restaurant, and Anika must have checked in on him a hundred times, but the guy was perfectly fine. My car had a dent, but what really bothered me was Anika fussing over him so much. Taking full advantage of the situation, he was acting all innocent. He might have grown up, but he was still as cunning as ever.

As we entered the restaurant, I parked my vehicle to the side and followed them in. Venkatramana stayed close to Anika, and they walked together like they were glued to each other. I wished I could leave as soon as possible.

We sat at a table, and just as I was about to order, Venkatramana interrupted, 'Anika likes chicken biryani. I'll have one as well.' He smiled while looking at Anika.

'What about you, Vikram?' he asked.

I want a knife to kill this bastard, but I stayed quiet.

I ordered some starters, and Anika and I chose Chicken 65. When the waiter served the food, Venkatramana, on his very first bite, offered it to Anika to taste.

'It's okay, Venkat, you have it,' Anika said, but after a couple of bites, she asked, 'So, what are you doing now?'

'Trying to go abroad for my master's,' he replied.

Bro, the guy who had backlogs his entire life wants to study abroad, while I'm stuck here with nothing—no film opportunities, nothing, I wondered.

'What about you, Vikram?' He pointed at me. 'Nothing.' He laughed. 'Man, you were the topper in our class,

and now… nothing?' He laughed like it was the funniest thing ever. I think that's what he wanted to hear.

Anika and Venkatramana talked for an hour. I neither listened nor wanted to be part of their conversation.

After lunch, we got ready to leave. I sat in the car, waiting for Anika to take her seat.

She walked back to the car, followed by Venkatramana. Like a gentleman, he opened the door for her. As she sat inside, she asked, 'Venkat, your number?'

She saved his number. It triggered something in me, even though I had nothing to do with it.

I didn't know why, but my anxiety was getting worse. I had no idea what to do after Anika took his number. My mind was a mess, just like before. If they started talking, I knew he would brainwash her soon. Was it even possible to be in a relationship with Anika again?

This thought had kept me awake for almost a week.

Not once did Anika try to call me about it. One fine day, I got a call from Arohi.

'I have great news!' she said, excitement in her voice. 'What is it?' I asked, barely interested.

'A famous producer wants to meet you. You got an offer!'

Tomorrow. Mumbai. I wasted no time and booked my tickets.

When I arrived in Mumbai, I headed straight to Bandra West, a place that housed some of Bollywood's biggest celebrities. Arohi was already there, waiting. She parked the vehicle and led me inside the apartment. But something felt different about her.

'You seem different,' I said. 'What's the matter?'

She smirked. 'Guess what? I have special news for you.' I raised an eyebrow. 'What is it?'

As we stepped into the elevator, she pressed the button for the fifteenth floor.

'I'm dating an actor,' she announced.

'What?! A twenty-two-year-old woman dating a 50+ actor?' I scoffed.

'Stupid! No! He's an actor's son. He's twenty-three and will be making his debut soon. And guess what? You're directing his film.'

I stared at her. 'Wait, what?'

'You heard me. I'm your co-director.'

I folded my arms. 'You called me here just to tell me about your boyfriend?'

'You don't get it. Big directors have been waiting to launch him. The entire industry has its eyes on him. But I chose you. Because no one balances mass and modern storytelling better than you. If you take this project and make it your own, you'll be a big name in the industry. This is the opportunity that can take you to the top.'

She was right. Who would pass on such an opportunity? After being rejected by dozens of producers, struggling through the streets, this was my chance. My one shot.

We finally reached the producer's flat. The door opened to reveal an old man with a clean-shaven face, holding a cigarette in one hand and a revolver resting on the table beside him. His entire apartment was filled with film posters.

'So, you're Vikram?' he asked, his eyes scanning me. 'What's your experience?'

I swallowed hard. I knew this would be another rejection.

'Nothing, sir,' I admitted.

He raised an eyebrow. 'Nothing? Then how did Khan refer you to me as a director?' He took a drag from his cigarette, exhaled, then walked over to the freezer. 'I don't know what's happening with this industry anymore. OTT platforms are taking over, young directors with low budgets are winning the game, and the Telugu film industry is leading the charts.'

Arohi stepped in. 'Sir, he's from Telugu cinema.'

The producer's eyes lit up. He walked towards us, holding a bottle of old whisky in his hand.

'Really?' he asked. 'Yes, sir.'

'Okay, we'll work soon,' he said, shaking my hand. 'When will you submit your script?'

'Sir, soon… in six months,' I replied.

He frowned. 'No, Vikram. We need to start shooting in three months. The entire audience is waiting. If we delay, we'll be trolled badly.'

I nodded. 'Okay, I'll have the script ready in two months. What genre are you looking for, sir?'

He sat down, deep in thought, before taking a shot of whisky. 'What about a mass entertainer?'

Arohi and I exchanged glances. We had already brainstormed something similar before.

'Sir, I'll write a naxalite backdrop, infused with objectivism.'

His face lit up. 'Perfect.'

Reaching into his pocket, he pulled out a chequebook and wrote an amount—₹15 lakh—as an advance. My hands trembled as I took it. My first income. The very thing I had dreamed of for years. For any middle-class man, this was life-changing.

'Congratulations, Director Saab!' Arohi teased as we headed out.

'Let's go to the bank. I have to share this with you,' I said.

'No, I'm not taking any of it,' she replied. 'Keep it. You need it more now.'

'I'm giving it to you. Let's go to the nearest bank,' I insisted.

She shook her head. 'No, I mean it. It's your film. I'll work for free.'

I smiled, overwhelmed by everything. 'I don't even know how to celebrate this moment.'

'Let's head to the beach,' I said.

The scent of salt filled the air, carried by a cool breeze that tangled through my hair. The rhythmic sound of waves crashing against the shore felt like a welcome, a soothing lullaby beneath the vast open sky. The golden sand stretched endlessly, warm and soft beneath my feet, tiny grains slipping between my toes as I took my first step forward.

The horizon was painted in hues of deep orange and purple, the sun slowly descending, casting a shimmering reflection over the restless waves. The water, a deep shade of blue, turned silver wherever the moonlight touched it. Far ahead, children laughed, running barefoot, their giggles blending with the whisper of the ocean. Couples sat quietly, fingers intertwined, lost in conversations only they understood. Street vendors lined the pathway behind us, their carts filling the air with the aroma of roasted corn, spicy bhel puri, and sweet, sticky cotton candy.

153

I inhaled deeply, letting the sea's presence settle inside me. This was more than just a place; it was a feeling. A reminder that time slows down here, that worries dissolve like footprints washed away by the waves.

I took a moment and dialled Mathura, as she was the only one who could celebrate more than I. I dialled her phone, but she wasn't picking up. I tried five times till I reached the airport. I even texted her, but she wasn't reading the messages, even though she was online and had uploaded a story about reaching the Taj Mahal with her friends. She might be busy, she'll call me later, I thought. Then I dialled my mother and sister, they were so happy for me. Anika called up and congratulated me.

I reached home, and Anika was at my house, waiting to congratulate me. She greeted me by warmly shaking my hand.

The moment I sat down to write, the weight of everything I had dreamed of finally settled on me. This wasn't just any script. This was my script. My first real film. And the words I put down on this page would decide whether I could actually become the director I had always wanted to be.

I started with a blank screen, staring at the blinking cursor. It was funny how an empty document could feel heavier than a full one. I had the story in my head—the clash of naxalism and objectivism, the ideological battle between collectivism and individualism—but bringing it to life felt like carving a mountain with a needle.

MY SHADOW KNOWS MY TEARS

Every morning, I locked myself in my small room, pushing distractions away. My phone stayed on silent, the notifications unchecked. I built a routine—writing from 7 a.m. to midnight, breaking only for coffee, occasional walks, and discussions with Arohi. She had become my sounding board, challenging my ideas, questioning my characters' motivations, and making sure I wasn't getting lost in the philosophy while forgetting the emotions that made a story worth telling.

Some days, words flowed like a river. Other days, I struggled for a single sentence. There were moments of self-doubt, moments where I wanted to tear everything apart and start over. But each time, I reminded myself—I had two months. And failure wasn't an option.

Mumbai moved on without me. My friends continued their routines, the industry kept churning out new films, and my name remained unknown—for now.

The producer had texted me twice asking about the progress.

Both times, I replied with a simple, 'Going great, sir.' In truth, I was struggling.

I had written the first act, introducing the protagonist—a young revolutionary raised in the heart of the naxalite movement, trained to believe that the system is the enemy. But then, he meets someone—a man who challenges everything he's been taught. An objectivist. A man who believes in the power of the individual, in self-reliance, in breaking free from ideology itself.

The clash wasn't just external—it was internal. I wanted my protagonist to go through hell, to break and rebuild himself through knowledge, through experience. To question everything and come out on the other side, stronger, wiser.

But writing this transformation wasn't easy.

Moving to Mumbai

I needed references. I spent nights watching documentaries on Naxal movements, reading firsthand accounts of rebels and intellectuals. I even visited an old journalist in Mumbai who had once interviewed former Naxal leaders. He told me something that stuck with me:

'You don't just leave an ideology; it leaves scars on you. It fights back. It never really lets go.'

That was it. That was the key to my story. Arohi noticed my exhaustion before I did.

'You need a break,' she said one evening, standing at my door with two cups of chai.

'I don't have time for a break.'

'Yeah? You also don't have time to die of stress, but you're doing it anyway.'

I sighed, rubbing my temples. She was right. But I couldn't stop now. I had finished sixty pages of the script. I needed at least 100 more.

So, I compromised.

Every Saturday night, Arohi and I went out to Marine Drive, to Juhu Beach, to some small café in Bandra where the lights were dim, and the world felt distant. We barely spoke about the film. She talked about her dreams, her past, and her random thoughts about life.

And in those small, stolen moments, I found clarity. At the six-week mark, the producer called me. 'Vikram, where are we?'

'Ninety pages in, sir. I'll be done soon.'

'Good. Because I told the press that we're announcing the film in a month.'

I froze. 'Wait. What?'

'We're doing a launch event. Posters, teaser shoot, everything. You have three weeks.'

My heart pounded, but I refused to panic. I had come too far to mess this up.

So, for the next twenty-one days, I disappeared from the world.

I wrote, rewrote, scrapped entire pages, and wrote again. Sleep became a luxury I couldn't afford. Arohi stopped arguing with me about the rest. She just made sure I ate, dropping off food at my place every evening.

Then, on the final night, at 3 a.m. I typed the last sentence.

I stared at those words for a long time. My hands trembled. Not with exhaustion, but with something else.

Relief. Pride. A strange kind of peace.

I sent the script to Khan with just two words: 'It's ready.'

Then, I collapsed onto my bed, closing my eyes, letting the world fade away.

For the first time in two months, I allowed myself to breathe.

The script was done. I had poured everything into it—my thoughts, my fears, my experiences—and now, there was no turning back.

I met the producer the next day at his office. The cheque for the advance was already in my pocket, a reminder that this was more than a dream. This was real. 'Vikram, you're not just the writer now,' the producer said, his voice surprisingly calm. 'You're the captain of this ship. The direction is your vision.'

I nodded, knowing exactly what he meant. The real test was now ahead of me—turning these pages into a film.

We started preparations. The clock was ticking. There was no time to waste. The three-month timeline was looming, and we had to move fast.

Khan's son was confirmed as the lead. He wasn't just any actor—he was the star. His brooding presence, the kind of intensity that made you think he could either conquer or destroy, was perfect for the role. But there was one problem: He wasn't an easy man to work with.

We met on the first day of the shoot. He stepped into the room, his eyes scanning everyone, his lips pursed in that familiar air of defiance.

'Director,' he said flatly. 'Let's see what you've got.'

I didn't flinch. I knew what I had to do. Khan's son wasn't the type to be coddled. He needed direction, but more importantly, he needed respect.

'Trust me,' I told him. 'I'm here to make your best performance possible. I know your strengths, and I know the story we're telling. Together, we'll create something bigger than all of us.'

He studied me for a long moment, and then, for the first time, I saw a flicker of understanding in his eyes. He nodded slowly.

'Let's do it.'

And that was the beginning of our collaboration.

The next two months were a blur. The shoot started with the first major scene—the introduction of the character of Khan's son, a naxalite turned disillusioned rebel. The camera was set up, the lights blinding, the crew bustling around. Khan's son stood there, silent, waiting for his cue.

I stood behind the monitor, watching his every movement, thinking through the scene in my head.

The director's chair felt like the weight of the world. But it also felt like I had finally found where I belonged.

'*The Revoken Naxalism*, take one!' I called out. The cameras rolled, and suddenly, the world around us became irrelevant.

There's a magic in directing—a quiet power that comes when you control every frame. I saw everything: his eyes, his body language, the way his silence spoke louder than words.

Khan's son wasn't just acting; he was becoming the character. And I was right there with him, guiding, shaping the performance, moulding the story.

But it wasn't all smooth sailing. The crew had its doubts, and there were clashes on set.

'There's too much philosophy,' one assistant director said during a break. 'This is a film, not a lecture.'

But I knew what I was doing. The ideological conflict had to shine through—it wasn't just for the plot; it was the story's soul. So, I pushed back. I reminded everyone that this wasn't a typical action film; it was a film about ideas, about what happens when two radically different worldviews collide.

'Mass appeal doesn't always mean compromising on depth,' I told the team. 'The audience will feel it if we stay true to the vision.'

As the days went by, I kept pushing forward. The intensity on set grew, especially when filming the scenes of the naxalite rebellion. There was a rawness to these sequences, and Khan's son's presence made them feel almost real. I directed with precision, making sure that each action, each movement, had meaning. Every scene had to serve the larger story of the individual versus the collective.

I spent hours discussing the philosophy behind the film with Khan's son. I wanted him to understand that his character wasn't just a rebel; he was a man of thought, someone who questioned everything.

The scenes became more complex as we moved forward. I had the crew practice the action scenes over and over, getting the timing and coordination perfect, while still staying true to the story's emotional core.

At the same time, we filmed the quieter moments—the moments of introspection—where Khan's son's character would wrestle with his internal conflict. These were the moments that I knew would make the film stand out, make it more than just an action flick.

The hardest part was integrating objectivism into the film. It wasn't just about quoting Ayn Rand or showing off some rationalist ideas. It was about making the audience feel that philosophy, letting them see the internal battle between collectivism and individualism through the protagonist's journey.

I pushed Khan's son to his limits. We worked together on the monologues, the moments where his character would argue with other figures in the film, figures that represented the opposing ideology.

I remember one of the more intense scenes: Khan's son's character, standing in the middle of a burning village, addressing a crowd of rebels. The speech was about freedom, about self-determination, about fighting not just for a cause, but for the right to think.

The first time we shot it, Khan's son struggled. It wasn't easy to bring such deep concepts to life in a moment of such chaos. But after a few takes, he found his rhythm. It was in his eyes—in the fury and passion that he brought to every word.

I watched it all unfold through the lens, knowing that this was what I had always wanted—to direct a film that didn't just entertain, but made people think.

The last day of shooting arrived, and with it came a rush of emotions. There was relief, yes, but also a deep sense of responsibility. This film was no longer just mine; it was the product of everyone's hard work.

'Vikram,' the producer said after the final scene was shot. He handed me a bottle of whisky, just like the first time we met. 'You did good work.'

I smiled, not knowing if I had done good enough, but knowing that I had given it everything I had.

And then, the long road ahead began—the editing, the sound design, the final touches. But I knew one thing for sure: In this film, the Khan's son, would make an impact. Whether it was the naxalite backdrop or the philosophical depth of objectivism, it was a story that would challenge its audience.

I was ready to face whatever came next, knowing that I had become more than just a director. I had become a creator.

Two months after the final shot was taken, the world finally saw the film. The anticipation was palpable, the press buzzing with excitement. The film was not just a typical action drama; it was an ideological clash, a battle of individualism versus collectivism, set against the backdrop of naxalism. People were curious. Could a film with such deep philosophical roots actually succeed?

When the film hit the screens, it was a storm. The audience poured in, curious to see this cinematic explosion of ideas. And they weren't disappointed. The story resonated with people on a level I hadn't anticipated. The action scenes were powerful, the philosophical dialogues striking, and the performance by Khan's son was nothing short of mesmerising.

The film didn't just run for a few weeks; it became a cultural moment. The box office numbers were astronomical. In the first week, it grossed nearly three times the initial investment—a number that few films in the industry could boast of. The film became a hit, not just because of its thrilling story, but because it made people think, and it stirred debate.

Word of mouth spread fast. People weren't just talking about the action; they were talking about the ideas. The naxalism vs objectivism debate had made its way from the screen into everyday conversations.

The success of the film didn't end with its box office run. Something unexpected happened—a ripple effect that I could never have predicted. Philosophy teachers, academics, and intellectuals started to take notice. They began encouraging their students to watch the Khan's son in the film not just for the sake of watching a movie, but as a tool for discussion.

Universities across the country saw an influx of students wanting to explore the ideas of objectivism and naxalism in greater depth. Professors used the film as a reference point for class discussions, analysing the core themes of individualism, freedom, and the consequences of blindly following ideologies.

One of the most memorable moments for me was when I received an email from a professor of philosophy at a prestigious university. He wrote:

> *'Dear Vikram,*
>
> *I wanted to take a moment to thank you for creating a film that has sparked a real conversation in my philosophy class. My students are not only discussing the characters but also engaging in debates on the concepts of self-interest and collective good. Your film has given life to the abstract, making it accessible and relatable. It's rare to see such an ambitious philosophical project in mainstream cinema. Please keep challenging the boundaries of thought and creativity. We look forward to seeing what you do next.'*

This was the kind of validation I never expected. *The Revoken Naxalism* was no longer just a film; it had become a philosophical movement. It wasn't just influencing pop culture but was also becoming a study material for young minds eager to question the world around them.

The media frenzy was also intense. Interviews, articles, and debates popped up everywhere. The film critics, who had initially questioned the possibility of combining high-octane action with deep philosophical themes, were now singing a different tune. They called it a game-changer for Indian cinema. One critic even referred to it as 'the most intelligent film to come out of Bollywood in the last decade.'

But the real success lay in how people engaged with the film. On social media, audiences were sharing their favourite lines, quoting dialogues, and debating the philosophical themes of the film in ways I had never imagined. People were watching it over and over, discovering new layers each time. The meme culture embraced it, making it a part of popular discourse.

> *'Watching The Revoken Naxalism is like opening a door to a new world. It makes you rethink everything you've been taught about society. I feel like I've been living in the Matrix and this film just woke me up.'*

The debate continued, not just in university classrooms, but in coffee shops, in homes, and on social media. People who had never considered philosophy were now discussing it in the same way they discussed the latest trends or TV shows.

For me, the success of *The Revoken Naxalism* wasn't just about the money or the accolades, though they were nice. It was about the impact. The film had bridged the gap between entertainment and education. It had turned philosophical ideas into something that could not only be understood but could ignite change.

The film didn't just succeed because of its action, or its big budget, or the star power of Khan's son. It succeeded because it had something more—substance. It made people think, made them question. It was a story about freedom, about the cost of ideologies, and about the power of individual thought.

And as the film continued to run, I realised something: This was just the beginning. I had made my mark in the industry, but more importantly, I had made my mark in the hearts and minds of people.

The Revoken Naxalism was no longer just my film. It had become a movement, a conversation, an awakening. And as the credits rolled on the final show of the film, I knew that this was just the start of something much bigger.

Time to Visit Jannaram

Just like the rest of India, I had become a well-known face in my hometown, a celebrity; more importantly, I was an eminent person for Anika, too. She used to come to my room just like Mathura usually did. I took a break from everything—the media, scriptwriting, the whole of Mumbai. I switched off my SIM.

Because Anika was with me, I wanted to have a few moments with her.

Anika picked up my bat. 'Let's play cricket. Could you teach me, Vikram?'

We reached the ground. I started bowling normally, but she was so bad at cricket that she couldn't even manage to hold the bat properly. I walked up to her, adjusted her grip, and then bowled five more balls. This time, she played well. 'Why don't we plan a trip?' Anika asked as we headed back.

'Goa? We missed it last time. Why don't we plan it now?'

'Goa is not for friends like us.'

'Then let's go to the forest! A three-day trip.' 'Let me ask a few of my friends in the department.' 'Nope. We'll go without permission.'

'There are tigers in there!' 'So what? Let's go.'

We packed our bags. I took a foldable tent, a sleeping mattress, and a folding chair. We headed towards Gate No. 2.

I stopped my scooty before the gate. It was a tiger reserve, and the guard wouldn't allow us to enter.

'We'll do one thing,' Anika said after a long wait. 'I'll distract the guard, and you keep moving forward. Once you're inside, just notify me—I'll jump over the chain.'

As per the plan, Anika walked slowly towards the guard. The guard woke up and headed to the washroom. That was my moment. I rushed my scooty forward. Anika jumped on before he could come back, and we passed him.

We were inside the forest. Tall, dense trees surrounded us.

We rode through PT Road. We had no idea where we were going, no destination, no signal, but one thing was clear—we were moving forward, deeper into nowhere.

By the time we reached the hilltop, it was a full moon night. We sat on the rocks, watching the moon. The special thing about the moon? It travels with us. Just like when we were kids, our mothers would feed us, pointing at the moon. Later, we'd grow up and praise our crushes, comparing them to it.

I set up the tent and laid out the inflatable sleeping mattress. I chopped some sticks with my knife and lit a fire. Then, I unfolded the mini-chairs and sat down. I took out the chicken I had brought from home, skewered it on a stick, and placed it over the fire.

The temperature kept dropping. It was almost 9 p.m. Anika wrapped herself in a sleeping bag. It was freezing, but the campfire kept us warm.

As we ate the roasted chicken, Anika took a bite and asked, 'Why isn't Mathura answering our calls or even replying to messages? I'm confused.'

'Not even mine,' I said.

'Yours too? I can't believe this.' 'Yeah, she might be busy,' I admitted.

'I don't think so, she is actively using Instagram.'

'Leave her. Look here, we got the mobile signal, it's one bar!'

'Yes, I have to dial Venkat. He would love this place.' A fire blew in my heart like a wave. I didn't know the reason behind it, but I wanted to kick that guy. Why did he come between our lives again?

She video-called him, showing everything, while he was openly flirting with her. I couldn't control myself and left the place.

I came back after a few minutes.

'Where had you gone?' Anika asked me.

'Toilet,' I answered and sat down. After a few moments, as my anxiety grew, I asked, 'is Venkat and you…in a relationship?'

She smiled and spoke, 'We are best friends, nothing more. He is my bestie.'

Who on earth invented the word bestie? I want to cut his—life is so cringe when someone says, he is my bestie, she is my bestie. It's damn irritating.

'What happened? Why are you so upset?' Anika saw my expression.

'Nothing!' I hesitated. 'Come on, just tell me!'

'Do you have feelings for anyone… just the way I have for you?'

'Yeah.'

'May I know who that is?'

'You'll never know what I'm talking about,' she blushed. 'Who?' I almost begged.

'The director.'

I stood up straight and ran towards the other side.

All my love had reached her. It was a whole decade of one-sided love. Never thought it could end this way. I couldn't control my emotions. I cried. I fell to the ground. Tears flowed down my face. All these years, my tears were blown away just like a gust of wind.

I gently opened my eyes, the moonlight lit my face, and I had a big smile on my face. I've never been happier…

these were the most precious moments of my life, making me feel something I had never felt before, never thought of, never imagined. It was like a daydream happening at night.

Suddenly, Anika's high-pitched screams shook me. I ran towards her. It was a leopard.

It was moving slowly towards Anika. She didn't move, just kept screaming.

I didn't know what to do for a moment. It was getting closer.

I couldn't move. I couldn't breathe.

My body became motionless, and my brain went blank. I think I took an overdose. All my love, all my efforts, all my pain were shattering in that moment.

I felt dizzy. My vision blurred.

The leopard was just five metres away from Anika. I fell unconscious, with a thud.

It echoed through the forest.

I woke up in Anika's arms. She was rubbing my hands. 'Are you okay, Vikram?'

I slowly stood up. 'What happened? Where was the leopard?'

'It ran away suddenly. It didn't do anything. It was just a mother protecting her cubs. Let's leave this place,' Anika said.

'No, we'll stay for two more days,' I replied, getting up. We talked about our childhood, our teachers, our classmates—everything. She was so happy during this time, and at one point, she smiled and said, 'I'm lucky to have you.'

It was getting late at night. We got up from our chairs to see how we could sleep, but there was only one tent. 'Anika, you sleep inside. I'll sleep outside with the sleeping bag,' I said.

'No, let's sleep together!' 'What?' I blushed. 'No, I mean, let's sleep in the tent,' she smiled.

Anika's beauty had a quiet elegance, the kind that didn't demand attention but effortlessly held it. Her skin, deep and rich like the earth after the first monsoon rain, glowed softly under the morning light. Even in sleep, she looked serene, her dark lashes gently brushing her skin, rising and falling ever so slightly with her breath.

I had woken up early, slipping out of the tent to search for neem sticks in the forest. The air was crisp, carrying the scent of damp leaves and distant blossoms. By the time I returned, Anika was still curled up, lost in dreams. Strands of her dark hair had fallen over her face, her lips slightly parted in the kind of peaceful slumber that made the world feel unhurried.

There was something so enchanting about her in that moment—serene, untouched by the weight of the day ahead. I paused, taking in the quiet prettiness of her presence, a sight that made the early morning feel softer, more meaningful.

I took a slice of bread and some jam, spread it quietly for her, and then played *Sundari Neeve* from my downloads.

I sat on a chair perched on the mountaintop. The view had everything—from the sunrise to rivers flowing through the forest—but now, it was turning foggy. As she woke up, I gave her a neem tree stick. She bit into it and scraped off the coating.

While she was still eating her breakfast, I packed everything and slung it over my shoulder. 'Let's go somewhere.'

'Where?' she asked.

'We'll go somewhere. Let's get to the scooty first, then we'll plan.'

We took our scooty and rode towards the forest. The sunlight was dim. I drove and drove, covering 8 kilometres, but I didn't find anything. I stopped at a place where there was a rocky hill, and we sat upon it.

Anika took a sip of Coke. 'So, what are your plans, Vikram?'

'I want to film an IAS role.'

'IAS?' She stopped sipping. 'No one will like that.' 'Yeah, Indian film audiences are mostly into mass entertainment, but... we'll see what happens.' 'Why did you choose that?'

'My father wanted to see me as an IAS officer, but that's impossible now. So, at least I can make a film on an IAS.'

She stood up and started walking. 'Come this way, Vikram. Let's go this way. I've heard something.'

The sound of water splashing reached our ears as we walked through the forest ahead.

MY SHADOW KNOWS MY TEARS

After walking almost 500 metres, we found something hidden behind the trees. I cleared the bushes with my hands.

It was a waterfall. We walked through, and Anika gently held my hand. We stepped onto the sand.

Water—the bond I never want to lose. Her presence healed a wound I had been carrying for over a decade.

The pain, the void—it all faded, washed away like a forgotten storm.

> *We often think that loving a person will*
> *ultimately hurt us the most, but for me,*
> *the pain lingered for years.*
> *The stars know my scars,*
> *My notes know my pain,*
> *My shadow knows my tears.*

Tears kept flowing as I tried to hide my face. My kerchief, unaware it was soaking up years of silent sorrow. My heart didn't know it could heal so soon, my eyes didn't realise this was the moment for them to shine. My soul didn't know that it would have a partner soon—someone who would understand the hopeful silence I lived with.

Even the flowing water didn't know it was easing my pain, and the breeze, so gentle, didn't know the burden it was lifting.

TEN

WATER (FALL)

~

I unfolded the chair and placed it in the water, and Anika sat on it.

We didn't speak. We just sat still in the silence of the forest. The wind blew through her hair, making a few strands dance over her face. She didn't bother tucking them away. The sound of the waterfall crashing down filled the air, blending with the rustling of leaves and the distant calls of birds.

The water flowed around our feet, cool and refreshing. Small ripples formed and disappeared, much like the unspoken thoughts between us. I glanced at her, but she was staring into the distance, lost in a world I couldn't enter.

I wanted to say something—maybe about the past, maybe about the way the golden sunlight made her eyes glow—but words felt unnecessary. Some moments were meant to be felt, not spoken.

A leaf floated by, spinning gently before getting caught in a small swirl of water. I watched it, wondering if we were just like that—two people caught in a current, moving together yet never truly knowing where we'd end up.

Anika finally broke the silence. 'Do you ever feel like time stops in places like this?'

I nodded. 'Yeah. And sometimes, I wish it would stay that way.'

She gave a small smile, one that didn't quite reach her eyes. The kind of smile that held more than it showed.

The sun dipped lower, painting the sky in soft shades of orange and pink. The air turned cooler, and the forest seemed to exhale with us.

I leaned back, letting the moment sink in. Because deep down, I knew—this silence, this stillness, this fleeting peace—was something we might never get again.

We reached the watchtower at the top of the hill, expecting a breathtaking view of the valley below. But as soon as we stepped inside, we froze.

A bear.

A massive, brown-furred beast lay curled in the corner, its heavy breathing filling the air. For a second, none of us moved. Then its eyes flicked open.

That was enough.

Without a word, we turned and bolted. I had never run so fast in my life. My heart pounded, my breath came in short gasps, and the branches scraped against my arms as we tore through the forest. Anika was right beside me, her laughter mixing with the rush of adrenaline.

When we finally stopped, panting and breathless, we looked at each other and burst into uncontrollable laughter. The fear, the thrill, the sheer ridiculousness of it all—it was too much. We collapsed onto the forest floor, clutching our stomachs as the echoes of our laughter faded into the evening air.

Three days later, we finally made it home, exhausted, sunburnt, and covered in scratches. But nothing could have prepared us for what came next.

The moment we stepped into town, we were met with glares. The forest department had been looking for us. Apparently, we had wandered into a restricted area—one we weren't supposed to enter. And the storm that hit while we were lost? It had triggered a full-blown search operation.

A forest officer stood in front of us, arms crossed. 'Do you have any idea how much trouble you two are in?'

I exchanged a quick glance with Anika. She bit her lip, trying to hold back a smile. I could still see the wild thrill in her eyes—the same thrill I felt.

'We, uh... got lost?' I offered, scratching the back of my head.

The officer wasn't amused. 'You were trespassing. And you could have been seriously injured—or worse.'

Anika finally spoke up, her voice softer now. 'We're really sorry. We didn't mean to cause any trouble.'

WATER (FALL)

After what felt like an eternity of lectures and paperwork, we were let off with a heavy warning and a small fine. As we walked away, Anika nudged me.

'Totally worth it,' she whispered. I grinned. 'Yeah, it was.'

Soon, my sister's wedding date was announced—it was fixed for twenty days later. As the date neared, the relatives started pouring into our home. My dad has lots of relatives, and so does my mother.

We set up a nearby function hall as the wedding venue. For the first time in years, I saw my mother truly happy. After so long, she finally had a smile on her face. Losing a partner you admire so much can push you into a depression so deep that no one can pull you out of it. My mother had been suffering from depression for many years. Along with her mental struggles, she also battled numerous health issues—thyroid problems, diabetes, and more.

Relatives started taking reels with me, and I almost felt like a mini-celebrity within my own family.

'Where is Mathura?' I asked Laxmi aunty.

'I don't think Mathura will attend the wedding,' she said, but deep down, I believed that she would.

'Let me call her.' I picked up my phone but hesitated. Instead, I took aunty's phone from her hand and dialled Mathura.

She picked up on the third ring. 'Amma?' she said, her voice soft.

'Mathura,' I spoke her name, and suddenly, her voice went pale. She didn't say anything for a few seconds. Then, she coughed.

'Vikram… how are you? Congratulations on your success.'

I didn't thank her. Instead, I said, 'Mathura, I'll book your flight tickets. Join us tomorrow.'

She didn't say anything. I could hear her breathing heavily—the kind of breath a person takes when they are crying. I didn't say another word.

She cleared her throat. 'Yeah… sure.' Then, she cut the call.

Since Anika had gone on a college trip, she would only be available the night before the wedding.

The wedding was about seven days away, but Mathura arrived earlier than expected, even though she initially planned to attend just the wedding.

We booked a nearby banquet hall and several hotels for the guests. I was constantly on calls, arranging everything—from the camera crew to the decorations—handling hundreds of people.

Then came the news that no bribe could silence—and with it, everyone's smiles evaporated.

I was sitting on the rooftop, gazing at the sky, when Mathura walked towards me.

'Vikram, why is everyone sad? Why are the relatives leaving?' she asked.

WATER (FALL)

I didn't respond. I just kept staring at the sky and the pond below, my emotions lingering in silence.

Everything was going well until the groom's family called us.

'We are cancelling the wedding,' they said. I asked them what the reason was.

'Someone from your family had a heated argument with one of our women. We want to be clear—we were looking for a respectable family with good people, not someone who spreads stupid rumours about our women. If this is happening now, what about tomorrow? It's not good. We are no longer interested in giving our son to your sister.' And just like that, everything fell apart. Relatives started leaving. My mother sank into depression again, and the happiness vanished from my sister's face.

Mathura didn't realise she was sitting beside me, resting her head on my shoulder as we watched the sunset in silence.

I felt there was nothing more for me to do. I hoped for the best and trusted that Krishna would never abandon us.

The next morning, I got a call from the groom himself.

'I'm really sorry for what happened. It was a misunderstanding. One of the girls from your side explained everything to us. We regret our decision. Please restart the arrangements. If you need anything, let me know.'

The mood was upbeat but a question lingered—we didn't want a guy who was so gullible, but we also wanted to find out the girl who fixed everything.

Mathura and I worked day and night to complete all the arrangements. Although she was working tirelessly with me, something about Mathura was off. Every time I spoke to her, her expression changed, her face shrouded in sadness.

I wanted to ask her if something was wrong, but I stayed quiet, hoping she would share when she was ready. That evening, I sat by the pond and called her over.

She came and sat at the edge, dipping her feet into the water.

'What's the matter? You've been acting weird these days,' I asked.

'It's nothing. Why did you call me here?' she said. 'Mathura, I just want to know what's wrong. Why do you seem so distant?'

She stayed silent. Suddenly, a tear rolled down her cheek.

'Come on, Mathura, don't be stupid. Just tell me.' 'I don't want to talk about it with you.'

'Hey, come on, speak out,' I insisted. 'Nothing. Please don't ask about it.'

Before I could push further, Anika suddenly appeared beside us.

'Surprise!' she said, hugging Mathura. 'How are you?' 'I'm good! How are you?' Mathura replied, forcing a smile.

Just then, her phone rang. It was her father.

'Hey, wait, Anika, I'll be right back,' she said as she left in a hurry.

I followed her, curious about what was happening.

Then, I saw him—Mohan uncle.

After two years, I couldn't help but hug him. It felt warm and familiar. He had been away, serving in the army, but in that brief embrace, it felt like no time had passed.

Mathura and Laxmi aunty stood frozen for a moment before emotion took over. Mathura's eyes brimmed with tears as she ran to her father, her voice catching as she said, 'Papa!' She hugged him tightly, as if making up for all the lost time. Laxmi aunty, overwhelmed, pressed her hands together, her lips quivering, before she stepped forward and held his face. 'You're finally home,' she whispered, her voice breaking. Then, unable to hold back any longer, she embraced him, tears streaming down her face.

As I stepped into the banquet hall, a sense of anticipation lingered in the air. The wedding hadn't started yet, but the space was already alive with murmurs of admiration. Mathura had handpicked most of the décor, and it's clear now—she had impeccable taste. Golden drapes cascaded from the ceiling, catching the soft glow of chandeliers. Rows of fresh jasmine and roses lined the entrance, their fragrance mingled with the crisp scent of new fabric and perfume.

The stage, adorned with intricate floral arches and twinkling fairy lights, looked straight out of a dream. Round tables draped in ivory cloth were neatly arranged, their centrepieces—delicate candles and orchids—drawing in compliments from every guest who walked in. Somewhere in the background, the wedding planners were making last- minute adjustments, waiters glided past with trays, and a few family members were already clicking pictures of the decor. Mathura's choices worked like magic—everyone loved them. I smiled to myself, taking in the beauty of it all.

Everything fell into place.

The marriage was solemnised as soon as the couple completed the seven rounds around the fire. In the evening, we had arranged for a mini-music extravaganza, where a few singers from TFI were performing. Thanks to my reputation in Bollywood, many prominent musicians agreed to be a part of it. As soon as the anchor announced the start of the event, the children stepped up to dance in groups as the crowd cheered them in anticipation.

Later, Anika took the stage. She signalled the music director to play *Raanjhanaa Hua Tera*, and the moment the song was played, she ran towards me. Before I could react, she pulled me up on stage by surprise. As we danced together, the entire crowd erupted in cheers. The energy was wild—whistles rended the air, and at one point, someone even threw money at us.

By the end of the night, almost everyone was convinced that we would be getting engaged.

The wedding concluded with the *vidaai*. While people witnessed these sombre moments keenly, a sense of sadness lingered in our family. After two decades of togetherness, one of us was leaving the home.

The groom sat inside the car, while everyone gathered around, waiting to bid goodbye.

Before leaving, he called me. 'Where is Mathura?' I was surprised. 'Do you know her?'

He smiled. 'She is the one who made this wedding happen. But I don't see her now—I wanted to thank her.' His mother interrupted. 'Let's go, we're getting late.'

And with that, they left.

I searched for Mathura everywhere but couldn't find her. Eventually, I spotted her father and rushed to him.

'Uncle, where is Mathura?'

He paused his call and looked at me. 'She left for Delhi. Didn't she inform you?'

I was stunned. 'But... why? And why has she been acting so strangely?'

Uncle sighed. 'I don't know. She hasn't been herself lately. She's not even behaving like my daughter.'

'How did she leave?' I asked.

'She took a cab to the airport. Her flight is at 4 a.m. I thought she told you.'

I didn't respond. Instead, I turned and ran home. Grabbing my phone, I quickly dialled Mathura. She didn't pick up.

I called again. No answer.

On the third attempt, her phone was switched off.

Suddenly, my phone rang back. It was Mathura. 'Vikraaaam...' she gasped, struggling to speak. Her breath was heavy, her voice shaky.

'Mathura! Are you there? What happened to you? Why do you sound like this?'

In the background, I could hear soft cries. My heart pounded. I didn't ask any more questions, just grabbed my car keys and rushed towards the airport.

The traffic was insane. The entire route was red—completely jammed. I weaved through every vehicle, desperate to move faster. But the expressway was at a standstill.

When I finally reached the airport, I called Mathura again, but her phone was still switched off. I rushed to enquire at the airport.

'Has the flight to Delhi taken off?' 'Yes, sir. It just departed.'

'When is the next flight?'

'In two hours.'

'I need a ticket.' I pulled out my ID and was about to hand over the cash when my phone rang.

It was Anika.

'Vikram, listen to me—Mathura is okay. Please come back fast. Everyone's waiting for you.'

I froze.

'What? How do you know?'

'Yes, I know, she just needs some space,' she insisted.

I stood there for a moment, torn and clueless. The panic began to ease—but the ache didn't.

Finally, I nodded to the ticket executive, pocketed my ID, and turned around. I had to trust her choice...even if I wasn't sure.

With a heavy heart, I headed back to my family.

Anika and I grew closer day by day. It had been almost three months since my sister's wedding, and together, we explored most of the places around us.

Finally, the day arrived—Anika was leaving for Hyderabad for her IT coaching, and I was heading to Mumbai to begin shooting my next film. A long-distance phase was beginning, and I was scared. What if this distance broke us again? I never brought up love between us after she accepted me once. I didn't want to make our attachment feel forced. I just wanted to maintain a balanced closeness, at least until marriage.

I took my flight and landed in Mumbai. My script was ready, only needing a few final touches.

I sat near my desk, trying to complete the climax, but my mind kept drifting. I picked up my phone and dialled Anika, just to let her know I had reached.

Her phone was busy.

I called her for the next few days, but every time it was the same—busy. At first, I thought she was talking to a friend. But in reality, she was on video calls with Venkat every single day. And like a fool, I never suspected anything.

The shoot began, but my anxiety grew worse every day. Long-distance was eating me alive. I couldn't control myself and often asked her, "Do you have someone else in my place? Are you avoiding me?'

She started restricting me—no pictures, no real conversations. Her replies became dry, distant, almost like I was forcing her to talk. It hurt. It hurt every single day. I couldn't focus on my shoot. I kept delaying it, waiting for the day Anika would finally talk to me properly.

Then one day, my anxiety took over. I asked her directly, 'What's going on between you and Venkat? Why are you talking to him so much? Are you planning to leave me?'

She snapped at me like never before. I calmed her down that day. But the next morning, I couldn't hold it in—I asked her again.

She never gave me a clear answer.

My mind spiralled. Every day, I had panic attacks and nightmares—dreams of Venkat picking Anika up for a wedding, of him kissing her.

I held up the shoot for fifty days, keeping a top actor waiting. The producer lost patience and gave me a final deadline of thirty more days, as the actor had other commitments. Somehow, I rushed through it, but honestly, I had no idea what I was even filming. My mind was drowning in Anika.

After so many struggles, we finally released the film. It was a disaster.

The audience hated it. The producer had invested ₹70 crores, but it barely collected ₹10 crores at the box office.

The entire Bollywood industry started to look down on me. The producers blacklisted me from filmmaking. My career was over in a jiffy.

After this failure, I quit filmmaking. I went home, completely lost, with no idea what to do next. If there was one thing I realised, it was that I should have been with someone good for my mental health.

My Return

One day, I decided to go to Hyderabad to meet Anika. Maybe seeing her would help me escape this depression, even for a while.

I called her. 'Hey Anika, can we meet tomorrow? Are you free?'

'Yeah, okay,' she said and cut the call within seconds.

Her voice felt distant, disinterested.

As we settled down on the sofa of a restaurant, I tried to make conversation. 'So, how's work going?' 'It's good.' Her reply was cold, indifferent.

'When are you coming back home?'

'Soon.'

I waited for her to continue, but she didn't. She was eating with one hand and texting on her phone with the other.

I stayed quiet, just watching her. 'How's uncle and aunt?' I asked.

This time, she put the phone on the table. 'They're fine.'

Suddenly, a message from Venkat popped up on her screen. She smiled as she replied to him.

'Anika,' I called her.

'What?' she responded, still typing, still smiling.

I clenched my fists. 'I'm talking to you. Can you stop texting that asshole for a second?'

Her face hardened. 'Why should I? He's my friend.'

'Then... what about me?' My heart pounded.

She looked at me straight in the eyes. 'You're also my friend.'

My heart stopped for a moment. A friend...was that all I ever was to her?

I swallowed hard. 'But...then why did you say you love me?'

She let out a dry laugh. 'I love you... as a friend. What are you even thinking? Just because a girl talks nicely to you, you assume it's a relationship? Senseless man.'

I felt my whole world crumble. 'Anika...please don't say that. Please... I beg you.'

She didn't answer.

She stood and quickly moved out of the restaurant. She didn't even look back.

And just like that, she walked away.

WATER (FALL)

I remained seated there, numb, staring at nothing in front of me. My body felt heavy, as if the weight of my grief had pinned me to the sofa. I wanted to stand up—but I couldn't. The reality of losing her had sunk in, wrapping around me like chains, keeping me stuck in this endless loop of pain.

My chest ached with an emptiness I couldn't put into words. My mind kept replaying every moment with her— the way she laughed, the way she spoke, the way she made me feel alive. And now, she was gone. I had lost her. The thought alone was unbearable.

Tears had long since dried on my face, but my heart still wept. I had cried incessantly, yet the pain of loss didn't lessen. It just sat there, a dull ache that was quite unbearable. My mother had seen me like this, her worried glances lingering longer than usual. She was dying every day, watching me this way, broken and defeated. But I had nothing to offer her, no words, no reassurances. I was barely holding myself together.

My life had virtually come to a screeching stop. The world outside continued as usual—people laughed, the sun rose and set, the clock ticked—but for me, time had stood still. I felt every bit of the loneliness. My heart knew pain and loss at the same time.

Anika came back home. I texted her for a five-minute meet, which she accepted.

We had a brief meeting.

'What? Why are you after me all the time? Can't you understand? I'm not in love. Why can't you just accept that?'

I broke down. Tears started to flow, yet again.

'Are you a child or what? Do you think you will get what you want by crying?'

'Please, Anika, don't leave me. I beg you. Please stay with me.'

'I'm not interested in this kind of drama. I'm moving abroad next week. Just understand—we can't be together, not even as friends. Keep that in mind.'

I bowed at her feet. 'Anika, please don't leave me. I'll wait for two years. Anika, please—"

She left. She didn't stop. She just walked away. She wasn't sad; she was brutally angry.

Suddenly, Mathura appeared from the back of the room.

She didn't say anything—just stood there.

My heart shattered. My cries wouldn't stop. I was falling, unable to hold myself together. Everything around me paused for a moment. Mathura walked towards me. I collapsed onto her lap.

I didn't cry anymore. I didn't look at anything. I just felt... Soon Mathu left Delhi for her semester exams.

I fell into depression, sinking deeper with each passing day. It wasn't just sadness—it was an emptiness that consumed me from within. Every thought felt heavy, every moment stretched endlessly, and no matter where I was, I felt lost. Sleep became both an escape and a torment, and waking up felt like a burden I wasn't ready to carry.

The things that once brought me joy now felt meaningless. Conversations became exhausting, and the world around me moved on while I remained stuck in a space where nothing made sense. I tried to distract myself, to push through, but the weight of my own mind pulled me back every time.

Loneliness wasn't just about being alone—it was feeling unseen, unheard, and disconnected even in a crowd. I wanted to talk, to explain what was happening inside me, but words failed. How could I describe a pain that had no shape, no clear reason—just an endless ache?

Some days, I wanted to disappear. Other days, I just wanted someone to pull me out of this darkness. But the hardest part? No one could. I had to find my own way back, even when I wasn't sure if I could.

Mathura came from Delhi, she saw me in this state, where I had lost almost 25 kg of weight, my body looked so weak...only a reflection of my earlier self. Everyone thought that this was because of the cinema, but how do I tell them someone whom I loved so much since my childhood went away from my life, ruthlessly breaking my heart into a million pieces.

I took my scooty and rode to the Zoological Park. I sat in total silence for hours. My body was still, but my heart was restless. I just stared ahead, watching the park, while my tears fell uncontrollably. I sat there until the sun disappeared behind the horizon, the darkness slowly swallowing the sky.

Then, I heard the sound of a scooty stopping nearby.

Mathura got down and walked towards me. She didn't say anything at first—just reached out and grabbed my hand.

'Let's go. It's getting late.'

I pulled my hand away immediately.

She grabbed it again, this time tighter. 'Leave me, Mathura. Just leave me. I want to stay here.'

'Your mother is worried about you. Aunty has been looking for you since morning—she hasn't even eaten.'

I didn't say a word. I just sat there, staring at nothing. 'Vikram... Vikram... Vikram...' She called my name five times, her voice growing more desperate each time. 'Why are you behaving like this?'

She tried to pull me up, dragging me towards the scooty, but I didn't move.

'Have you lost your mind, Vikram?' she snapped. 'She's just a girl! Why are you ruining yourself every single day, while she's having a great time with Venkat?'

Hearing his name made my blood boil, but I remained silent.

Mathura grabbed my hand again. 'Come on, Vikram!' Something in me snapped. I yanked my hand away and, before I could even think or stop myself, I slapped her.

'Can't you see how much I'm suffering?' I yelled. 'Can't you understand that my heart is shattered? I'm struggling to breathe, Mathura! Anika is mine—I can't accept the fact that she left me. How could she make such a decision so easily? Am I wrong? Am I not deserving of love?'

Tears streamed down my face as I broke down. 'I've cried and cried... and she walked away like I was nothing.' Mathura didn't say anything. She just turned and left.

I slumped onto the wooden bench, staring up at the night sky. The Zoological Park was surrounded by trees on all sides, with only a road passing through. The world around me felt empty, just like the hollow ache in my chest. The night stretched on like an unbearable eternity.

The wind whispered through the trees, carrying the distant sounds of the forest—crickets chirping, dry leaves rustling, the occasional cry of an unseen bird. But none of it reached me. I was alone, trapped in a silence that belonged only to me and my grief.

Her memories clung to me like shadows—Anika's smile, the way she looked at me, the warmth of her presence that once felt like home. Now, all of it was just an echo, a ghost that refused to leave. I closed my eyes, hoping for sleep, for a brief escape. But the moment my eyelids shut, she was there—laughing, holding my hand, looking at me with eyes that once held meaning.

And then, just as quickly, she was gone. With him.

A sharp pain spread through my chest, tightening like a fist around my heart. How could she? How could she leave so easily, while I lay here, breaking piece by piece? Did she ever love me? Or was I just another passing moment in her life, forgotten as soon as it ended?

Tears burned in my eyes, but I was too exhausted to cry. I had cried enough. Now, there was only emptiness. A hollow space where love once lived.

The night grew colder. The stars above shone indifferently, as if mocking my suffering. The world moved on.

Anika moved on.

But I remained here, stuck in this never-ending night, haunted by a love that was never meant to last.

I curled deeper into myself, wrapping my arms around my chest as if that could stop the ache. But nothing could.

Nothing would.

Mathura was standing over me. I didn't realise when she came again.

'How many days are you going to do this, Vikram?' Her voice was firm, but there was pain in it. 'How many days?'

I didn't answer.

'Do you think you're the only person in the world who's ever loved someone? The only one who's ever been heartbroken?' She crossed her arms, staring at me with frustration and concern. 'Your mother is waiting for you. She hasn't eaten anything ever since you left home. You're not alone, Vikram. You have people who care about you.'

'Leave me, Mathura.' My voice was hollow. 'I just want to stay here. Let me be. I've lost everything. I can't sleep. I can't stay. I just want to rest here forever. I want to quit everything.'

She knelt beside me, her voice softening. 'Vikram, this isn't the answer. You have family. You have a future. You're not alone. Nothing is over yet. You have your whole life ahead of you.'

I gave her an aggressive look. 'If you had ever truly loved someone, you wouldn't say these things.'

She sighed and looked away for a moment, then turned back to me, her eyes filled with something I couldn't understand.

'I have loved someone, Vikram. Don't ever say that I haven't.'

Mathura took a deep breath, then said the words I never expected to hear.

'I love you, Vikram.'

My heart stopped, I didn't face her, I didn't want to. I lifted my head slowly, my vision blurred with tears. Mathura stood there, her eyes filled with something I couldn't decipher—anger, frustration, or maybe pain. The weight of her words pressed against my chest, but I couldn't respond. I was exhausted, broken beyond repair.

'I love you, Vikram,' she said, her voice trembling.

For a moment, everything stopped. The wind, the rustling leaves, the distant hum of the city—everything faded into silence. Her words hit me like a wave, but I was too lost to feel their warmth.

I stared at her, unable to process what she had just said. Love? Love was what had destroyed me. Love was why I was here, drowning in my own misery. Love had taken everything from me.

She stepped closer, her fingers reaching for mine, but I pulled away. I didn't deserve this. Not now. Not when my heart still belonged to someone else.

'Don't,' I whispered, my voice barely audible. 'Don't say that, you saw that I'm broken, and now you're just trying to calm me down, right? Please don't do that, Mathura.'

'Why?' she asked, her voice breaking. 'Because you only see her? Because you think no one else in this world could love you?'

I let out a shaky breath, my tears falling freely now.

Mathura wiped her own tears away, her voice trembling as she spoke. 'Since childhood, you were my entire world, Vikram. Do you remember those nights? The way we watched films together, the times we fell asleep on the same bed, the way you always protected me like I was something precious?'

'I wrote a whole book on you, and you never even realised. I love you, Vikram. And my heart knows how many years I've carried this love in silence. I know you've loved Anika since school…but you never saw me. Not even once.'

Her voice cracked, and she swallowed hard, forcing herself to continue. 'Do you know how many times I tried to make you notice me? How many times I stood in front of you, dressed in my best, hoping you'd just look at me the way you looked at her? But you never did. You only saw her.'

Her shoulders trembled. 'I have no world outside of you, Vikram. No one. I never let any man into my heart except you and my father. And now, he won't be with me every day, and you still won't see me.'

She took a deep, shaky breath, her fists clenching. 'When Anika came into your life, I accepted it. I thought, maybe, for once, you had found happiness. And if that meant I had to step back, I would. But I couldn't bear to watch it. So, I ran. I disappeared, hid my tears, pretended to be fine.'

Her breath hitched, and her voice dropped to a whisper. 'On the day of your sister's wedding… I stood right behind you, Vikram. When you picked up your phone to call me, I was there. Watching you, breaking inside. But I couldn't stay. I couldn't let you see me fall apart. I turned around… and I left. I took the first flight out because I knew if I stayed any longer, I wouldn't be able to let go.'

Her eyes, raw with unshed tears, met mine. 'And now, you're the one breaking. And I can't watch it, Vikram. I can't.'

Her voice shattered on the last word, and she turned away, as if afraid I'd see the depth of her pain. But I already had. And I didn't know what to do with it.

I didn't say anything. I just left for home without looking back at her. That night, I lay on my bed, silent, not even speaking to my mother.

But my sleep didn't last long.

Suddenly, my mother burst into my room, panting heavily.

'Vikram! Vikram, wake up! Wake up!' Her panicked voice jolted me awake.

I sat up, alarmed. 'What happened, Amma? What's wrong?'

She took a deep breath, trying to steady herself, but her words came out in broken gasps.

'Mohan uncle… Mohan… he was attacked by terrorists—' She stopped, choking on her words.

My heart dropped. Without another thought, I ran toward Mathura's house.

When I reached, I saw her.

She was sitting in the corner of the hall, broken. Silent.

But this… this wasn't the Mathura I knew.

I had seen her like this only once before—when she was a child, curling up in the same corner, lost in thoughts of her father. Whenever Mohan uncle was away at the border, she used to sit there, hiding her pain from the world. She always hid her anxiety, her fear—she had prepared herself for this moment, knowing deep down that one day, her father might not return.

But now that the moment had arrived, she wasn't the same.

Mathura had no one else.

She had no ties with her mother's family. No ties with her father's family. Their entire family had been broken ever since her parents' love marriage. She had only ever had two people—her father and me.

And now... she had only one.

I stood there, watching her, my chest tightening. I didn't know what to say.

Two Months Later

Mathura and I were on the train. She sat by the window, staring blankly outside. She hadn't come out of the pain that had struck her. Her eyes were empty, lost. She folded her arms and rested her face on them, not moving, not speaking.

For two months, she hadn't uttered a single word. And I... I hadn't tried either. I was drowning in my own grief— Anika's absence had wrecked me. My life had become a blur, a series of endless days with no meaning. I didn't even know how many times I had gone to buy groceries or picked up medicines for my mother. Everything felt the same.

The train rattled forward, but Mathura never tilted her face. She remained still, frozen in her sorrow.

I hadn't informed her mother that we were travelling to Kerala. I knew she would stop us if she knew. Her family were Namboothiri Brahmins, one of the highest castes in

Kerala, while her father, Mohan uncle, belonged to the Pulaya community, one of the lowest castes, traditionally agricultural labourers. Caste had been one of the biggest reasons her father's marriage had been rejected by both sides of the family. Mohan uncle, being in the Army, was another reason.

The train pulled into Kochi Station. I gathered our luggage, but Mathura remained the same, unmoved. I nudged her gently, signalling her to follow. Without a word, she stood up and walked behind me.

I booked a hotel near the beach, and the next morning, we set out for Vypīn Island, where Mohan uncle's parents had once lived.

As we stepped onto the island, the salty breeze carried the scent of the Arabian Sea, mingling with the rich aroma of Kerala's backwaters. The place had an air of quiet resilience, as if time had stood still here.

I tried to locate their house, but my memory was hazy. As we wandered through the narrow streets, I spotted a middle-aged man walking towards us.

'Uncle, do you know where I can find Madhavan & Saraswathi's house?'

He scanned us for a moment, suspicion flickering in his eyes. *'Kudumbam snehithanmaar? Njan ningale munnil kaanilla, evideya?'*

The words didn't sound like English.

'Sir, could you speak in English?' I asked. 'Where are you from?' His doubt deepened.

WATER (FALL)

'We're from Telangana,' I said.

Before I could say more, Mathura suddenly collapsed beside me.

She hadn't eaten anything since we had left.

Panic surged through me. I quickly pulled out a bottle of water and splashed it on her face, but she didn't wake.

The man stepped forward, signalling towards a nearby clinic. *'Avale asupathriyilekku kondu pookaam.'*

He took my luggage and guided us towards a small clinic, tucked between coconut trees. It wasn't a typical hospital—just a house, converted into a place for treating the sick.

A frail old man, his spine slightly bent, walked out of a room, a stethoscope draped around his neck. He placed it on Mathura's chest, listening carefully.

After a moment, he turned to me and spoke in English. 'She's fine. There's nothing to worry about. I've given her glucose—she just needs rest.' Relief washed over me.

'Where are you from?' he asked.

'Sir, we're from Telangana. We're here looking for Madhavan and Saraswathi, who lived here in the 1990s.'

The man studied me carefully. His expression changed. 'I'm Madhavan,' he said. 'What do you need?'

I took a deep breath, bracing myself. 'Sir... Mohan... he was your son, right?'

The moment I spoke those words, tears welled up in my eyes.

'He… he is no more.'

Madhavan's body swayed. He looked as if the ground beneath him had disappeared. Just as he was about to collapse, I caught him.

A painful cry tore from his lips. His wails echoed through the house, drawing the attention of the entire neighbourhood.

His wife came rushing in, alarmed.

'What happened? Why are you crying?' she asked. Madhavan barely managed to whisper, 'Mohan *ini illa.*'

(Mohan is no more.)

Her face went pale. A moment later, a heartbreaking scream escaped her lips. She broke down, tears flowing uncontrollably.

Mathura and I sat on the sofa, watching her grandparents crumble under the weight of the news.

There were no words left to be spoken. Only grief.

'We lost Mohan when he left us. It was my mistake—I opposed his marriage to a Brahmin woman. I didn't just oppose him—I threatened him to stop loving her. But my son… in twenty-three years, he never retaliated. He stayed silent. I was so brutal—I dragged him out of this house. My ego, my pride… they destroyed everything. I lost the only son I had. I've regretted it every day for the past twenty years. I even tried to find him, but failed each time. How do you know my son? Who are you?'

WATER (FALL)

'She is your granddaughter,' I said, pointing towards Mathura. Granny came in and hugged Mathura, and both of them broke down in tears.

They had two children, Mohan and Harika. While Mohan left home, Harika died in a car accident right after her marriage. These two elderly parents became orphaned parents. Many people tried to approach them, pretending to care and laying claim to assets... everyone invariably betrayed them. Madhavan had completed his post-doctorate in medicine and, once upon a time, was one of the top surgeons in Kerala.

That's why Mohan uncle wanted Mathura to sit for NEET. To everyone's surprise, she cracked it—AIR 22—and got admission in AIIMS Delhi.

It was clear that Mathura's entry had brought light back into their lives. They were overjoyed. They served the richest food I'd ever eaten. Mathura's face lit up with a smile—I had never seen her so happy, not even in my childhood. Almost everyone from the colony came to meet Mathura, and her grandparents arranged a party for everyone.

The next evening, he took us to the Marine Drive, the sun was setting in the west, painting the sky in shades of orange. We sat at the edge of the cobbled pavement, our feet dangling above the sea. A few metres behind us, three youngsters were playing the guitar. I sat a little apart, watching as they joked and laughed with Mathura, who understood Malayalam. They looked happy.

I closed my eyes and lay on the road, staring up at the sky. As I suffered through my memories, tears began to flow back. My heart pounded heavily—I wanted to fix this. I couldn't control the pain that had consumed me. I craved it, yet I was broken. In the quiet space, I didn't want to disturb their moments of happiness. Later, they returned. Mathura woke me up. It's the 31st. Let's go to Jew Town. Grandpa said it's a special night.

As the clock inched towards midnight, we arrived at Jew Town on New Year's Eve. The narrow streets, usually quiet, had a different energy tonight—soft laughter echoed, and the scent of spices mixed with the cool night air.

The Paradesi Synagogue stood still in time, its ancient walls watching over a world that had changed. Mathura walked ahead, her fingers grazing the old wooden doors of an antique shop, while her grandmother looked around with a nostalgic smile.

Madhavan, who was driving us through the dimly lit lanes, spoke softly. 'Once, these streets bustled with Jewish traders celebrating their own festivals. Now, time has left only whispers of the past.'

We reached the waterfront just in time. The backwaters stretched endlessly, reflecting the golden glow of distant fireworks. The first spark of midnight light burst in the sky, and for a moment, the past and present felt beautifully intertwined.

As we walked through Jew Town on New Year's Eve, the air was filled with the aroma of spices and freshly baked bread. Small cafés and stalls lined the streets, offering everything from crispy banana fritters to steaming cups of chai.

Near the waterfront, we spotted a large tree wrapped in thread lights, glowing softly against the night sky. It stood tall, its golden light reflecting on the cobbled streets, adding a magical charm to the old town.

Madhavan led us to a small eatery, where we feasted on Malabar biryani, *meen pollichathu* wrapped in banana leaves, and soft appams with coconut stew. Each bite carried the essence of Kerala—rich, flavourful, and comforting.

We savoured warm payasam in clay cups while watching the fireworks light up the backwaters. Under the glow of that tree, surrounded by history, good food, and laughter, the night felt timeless.

Sometime later, a giant Santa Claus effigy (*Pappanji*) was burned.

'The burning of the Pappanji symbolises letting go of the past year's hardships, negativity, and bad experiences, making way for a fresh and happy start to the new year,' Grandpa explained.

Our feast continued… the next morning, the dining table was laden with dozens of aromatic breakfast dishes. Mathura was helping her grandma in the kitchen. Grandpa entered the dining room, dressed in his dhoti and white shirt. During breakfast, we shared our plan to visit Mathura's mother's side of the family. They didn't say anything at first—they remained silent.

Grandpa adjusted his glasses and agreed. We took grandpa's old Rolls-Royce from his garage and headed toward Tripunithura.

We took a wrong turn but finally reached the house. It was a two-storey structure with old architecture. I quickly opened the door for Mathura. Her eyes were glowing—she had only seen this building in pictures shown to her by her mother. There was a coconut farm inside and a beautiful garden right in front of the house.

We knocked on the door, and a little child opened it. 'Who are you?' she asked in an Indo-American accent.

'Is this Janaki's house?'

'Yeah... Grandma!' she called out and spoke in Malayalam, '*Aarengilum vannittundu!*'

'What is she saying?' I asked Mathura. 'Someone has come,' she translated.

An old woman walked towards us, adjusting her glasses. 'And you are...?'

'Grandma, I'm Laxmi's daughter,' Mathura said, hugging her.

Tears fell from grandma's eyes. 'It took twenty years for you to realise you have a grandmother. Why does your mother have so much ego? Why didn't she come back in just two months? We searched everywhere in the state. We lost our respect. People whispered that our daughter ran away with a lower-caste man. I never understood—aren't all humans equal? Karma punished me with loneliness. All my sons and daughters lost their mother while building their careers in other countries.'

She let us in. We sat on the sofa as a woman in her 30s came towards us—it was Mathura's aunt. After spending a few hours, we took their leave and came back to the grandparents' home.

Later, at dinner, grandfather and grandmother were busy placing food on the dining table. We took our seats, and they joined us.

'We were planning to take you to our place,' we said.

At first, they didn't answer. They just looked at each other.

'Yes, we will come,' Grandma finally smiled.

Smiles spread across everyone's faces as we headed towards Jannaram. We didn't tell anyone that we were arriving.

When we reached Jannaram, our entire colony gathered around our car—it was the first time a Rolls-Royce had entered our neighbourhood. I honked, but aunty didn't come out. We entered the house, and I rang the doorbell as everyone followed me.

Aunty stepped out, and her body froze at the sight of her mother. She was stunned and pleasantly surprised, as she covered her mouth in awe and disbelief. She bent down, touched her mother's feet, hugged her tightly and cried.

'I'm sorry, Maa. I never thought I could leave you. Mohan gave me everything. He always took care of me, but I couldn't make it up to you.'

Both of them sobbed, holding onto each other. Meanwhile, granny and grandfather folded their hands in apology.

Two Days Later

Aunty, overwhelmed with joy after reuniting with her parents, broke down many times. But her mother stood by her like an angel, protecting her constantly. Though inconceivable, grandfather expressed a desire to stay back in Jannaram for a while, perhaps permanently.

'I think I'd like to practise again,' he said one evening. Soon, he joined a nearby hospital. Slowly, both grandparents began adjusting to life in Jannaram. They started treating Laxmi aunty as her own daughter, making up for years of silence and separation.

Mathura, meanwhile, was finally surrounded by love— her cousin, extended family, and the warmth of a complete home. She began to smile again, a little brighter each day.

'Anika, I know it's easy to hate me, but I still love you—always have, always will. Please accept me as your boyfriend again—I beg you. I'm sorry for asking about your personal matters that day, but you're the only one I have. Please, Anika, don't ignore this message.'

I typed this and hit send—I sent this message a hundred times.

But there was silence on the other end. I couldn't accept that she was gone. She had always been my priority, through all these years and months. I even put my film aside just to pursue Anika, in the hope of reviving our relationship.

My brain was constantly overwhelmed with her thoughts. I couldn't sleep. I couldn't function normally. Sometimes, her memories hit me like an electric shock—I kept thinking if only I had made a good film, maybe she could have stayed. I should have cared more, done more. Eventually, I slipped into depression.

On the outside, I spoke normally with everyone. But when I was alone, my thoughts tormented me. I would break down, shouting at nothing, unable to bear the silence.

One fine day, Laxmi aunty entered my room. 'Vikram, what's happening? What are these sounds?

Why are you crying so badly? What's going on, Nana?' 'Nothing, aunty,' I said, holding back my tears.

'I know everything,' she said gently. 'Mathura told me. I know it hurts when someone walks away after you've carried that love in your heart for a decade. But I can't bear to see you like this.'

She walked over, poured a glass of water, and handed it to me. She sat down near me on my bed.

'Look, Vikram, suffering is personal—you carry it alone. But when someone leaves, it's not always your fault. It's their choice. Maybe they thought they'd be better off elsewhere.'

'But it's my fault. I shouldn't have brought up her personal life. I loved her so much. Maybe it's my mental health, or maybe something else. But I lost her. And now I regret everything.'

She looked at me for a long moment. 'Vikram, what do you mean by love?' 'Caring for someone through their entire life.'

'That's just a film dialogue,' she said. 'True love is staying with someone through their changes, through thick and thin of life. Accepting the new versions of them wholeheartedly. Understanding their struggles and helping them through their confusion and indecision in life. That's love.'

I didn't say anything.

'I can't see you like this, Vikram. I have to tell you something. It might change your relationship with Mathura forever. But she has loved you since childhood.'

She got up from the bed and sat on the chair.

'I don't know how to say this, Vikram. You are everything to her. Will you—'

I raised my palm before she could say that word.

'No, aunty. I can't. No one else can take that place in my heart. I value our friendship too much to ruin it. I'm not worthy of her. I can't give her a future. I'm… I'm nothing right now.'

'She's doing her postgraduate studies. She'll be a surgeon soon. We expect nothing from you, Vikram,' she said sadly.

'If you ask me to marry her, I will. I won't say no— because I respect you more than anyone. But I'd be doing it without love. Anika owns my heart. I can't give it to anyone else.'

'Vikram, you are our strength. You gave us light when we had nothing. Please, marry my daughter.'

'Aunty, please, I can't do that. I can't see her in that place.'

My mother entered the room. 'Vikram, you have to accept this.

Some doors in life don't close because we lock them.

They stay open because we're afraid to walk away.'

Present Day

The pages ended. I was confused—what could the ending be? I immediately took a bus to Chandrapur—not just to write the ending, but to know it. To understand the story. Love, in its truest form, is not merely an emotion but a fundamental expression of existence. It's not something that happens to us; it's something we create, something we choose, something we become.

Philosophers have long debated whether love is an accident of emotions or an act of the will. Plato saw love as the soul's longing for beauty and truth, an ascent from physical attraction to the love of wisdom itself. Aristotle believed love was found in deep friendship, where two individuals wish the highest good for each other. Spinoza argued that love is the joy we feel in recognising another as an extension of our own essence.

In existential thought, love is not destiny but a conscious engagement with another being. Sartre saw love as a struggle between freedom and possession—when we love, we desire the other's presence, but true love must respect their autonomy. Camus, in his absurdist philosophy, suggested that love, like life itself, has no inherent meaning except the one we give it.

From an objectivist perspective, love is the ultimate recognition of values in another. Ayn Rand argued that love is not self-sacrifice but self-affirmation—the admiration of someone who reflects our deepest ideals. It is not about losing oneself but about finding someone who amplifies what we already are.

Ultimately, love is not a mystery to be solved but a reality to be lived. It is not just about passion or permanence, but about understanding and growth. To love is not to complete another, nor to be completed, but to walk alongside them—not as halves seeking to be whole, but as whole beings choosing to share the journey.

I reached the hospital but couldn't find her. I searched everywhere, but she was nowhere to be found. I headed to the reception.

'Where is Dr Mathura?' I asked.

'She comes here occasionally. She lives in Delhi. By the way, what's your name?'

'Vasu. Why?'

He handed me a diary, its vintage cover worn with time. 'She told me to inform you that the ending is written in this.'

I took the diary and walked towards a park.

Sitting on a bench, I crossed my legs, opened the diary, and began flipping through the pages.

14 September 2015: Vikram's Birthday

I had brought special chocolates from Delhi and ordered a cake.

12 A.M.

I knocked on his door, but he didn't wake up. I sat on his balcony, waiting for thirty minutes, then knocked again. Still, he didn't open the door—maybe he was in a deep sleep. I waited another half an hour. The winter chill was at its peak, and the temperature kept dropping, but I wanted to celebrate this moment with him. I waited another half an hour, but he still didn't open the door.

At 5.30 a.m., aunty came to the verandah and saw me sitting near the steps.

'Mathura, you haven't worn a jacket! Why are you here? When did you come?' She rushed towards me and touched my hand. 'It's so hot...' She touched my cheek. 'You have a fever! Let's go home. Come with me. Why are you roaming in the cold?'

'Aunty, it's Vikram's birthday. I want to give him these chocolates and the cake.'

'We can give them to him later. Your body is burning up.

Please, let's go home.'

'No... let's give this to him first.'

Aunty sighed, then walked up to the door and knocked heavily. Vikram finally woke up and opened the door, his eyes half-open with sleep.

I placed the cake on the table. He swiftly cut the cake, shook my hand, handed me a piece, and then walked back inside.

This birthday was memorable for me, not because of the celebration, but because I had seen love in the coldness.

I flipped to the twenty-fifth page, as all I wanted was the story that followed.

My heart broke when I saw Vikram lying on the ground. His father was no more.

He had always told me that he wanted to drive his father around in his own car one day, that he dreamed of flying him in his own private jet. Uncle meant everything to him.

I closed the diary for a moment, letting the weight of those words settle. The evening air in the park was cool, rustling the pages in my hands. My fingers traced over the ink, over the memories Mathura had poured into these pages—of love in the cold, of silent heartbreak, of dreams that would never be fulfilled.

Taking a deep breath, I flipped to the next entry.

2 March 2017

'Vikram hasn't spoken much since uncle passed away. His eyes look empty, as if the world around him has lost its meaning. I tried talking to him today, but he just nodded and walked away. I miss his old self—the one who dreamed big, who laughed loudly, who made me feel like I belonged.

I know grief changes people, but it feels like he's slipping away, and I don't know how to bring him back.'

I exhaled slowly. The Vikram I knew now—was he still carrying this weight? Had he ever let himself grieve properly?

I turned to another page.

5 January 2022

Vikram, if you're ever reading this—

I hope you know that even when you pushed everyone away, I never left. Even when you shut yourself off, I still waited. I don't know what the future holds, but if there ever comes a day when you feel alone, when you feel like no one understands, please, just remember.

You were never alone. Not even for a second.

I shut the diary, my chest tightening. The park lights flickered above me, casting long shadows. The night was silent, except for the distant hum of traffic.

For the first time in years, I felt something shift inside me. Maybe it was regret. Maybe it was longing. Or maybe—just maybe—it was the realisation that someone had always been waiting for him to come back.

And maybe it wasn't too late.

'Some love stories never find a home. They wander, they wait, they linger in the corners of our hearts until time forces them to fade.'

I closed the diary, my heart sinking.

Not every love story has a happy ending. Some are just echoes of what could have been.

But Mathura had written this story for a reason. Maybe it wasn't about finding an ending. Maybe it was just about being seen, even if it was too late.

I looked up at the night sky.

Maybe love was never about being chosen. Maybe it was about loving anyway.

And maybe that was enough.

WATER (FALL)

Saturday

This was the day I confirmed that the new girl in our colony, Anika, was none other than your Anika. My tears fell the moment I realised it, and I ran inside the washroom so that no one could see me cry. When I came back and saw you both together, it pained me very much. I couldn't move. I was sleepless all night. The next day, when I saw you both happy, I just wanted to leave—to step away and let you be happy together.

That night, I looked into Anika's story—about the time you both trekked through the forest. I cried a lot. Not because you were happy, but because I wondered—why wasn't I in Anika's place? I stopped answering your calls. Every time I heard your voice, my heart grew heavier, and my tears wouldn't stop.

I hope you never read this.

It was our wedding week. I was so happy that Vikram was going to be mine, yet sad that he didn't even like the fact that love could happen twice.

One night, he spoke to me and confessed that he was being forced into this marriage, and had no interest in going through with it. But I believed that sometimes, even forced situations could lead to a beautiful life. I promised myself that I would show him all the love I had kept hidden all these years. I would take care of him in every possible way.

Three days before the wedding, I was discussing the arrangements with the manager when the sound of a bottle crashing hit my ears. I rushed outside and saw Vikram, completely drunk. His eyes were bloodshot, and his body had collapsed. I had never seen Vikram drink before, not even a single sip of alcohol. But that night, he was someone else entirely.

With the manager's help, I carried him to bed. I didn't tell anyone. I just wish that our wedding day would come soon, so that he would find relief from his pain. I wish I could be his healer. I wish I could bear this pain instead of him.

The next morning, he woke up, and I was sitting beside his bed. He looked at me, then sat up in silence. He didn't say a word.

He walked into the bathroom, bathed, and came back—still feeling nothing. His face was pale, his eyes red. He wasn't himself. He wasn't the Vikram I knew.

Wedding Day

He took the vehicle and left the wedding venue. He said he would return very soon.

The mirror reflected a bride, 'But was it me?'

The morning light streamed through the curtains, casting a soft glow over the room. I sat before the mirror, watching as the makeup artist delicately traced the brush along my cheeks, blending the foundation to perfection. My skin felt cool under the touch of her fingers, the scent of roses and sandalwood lingering in the air.

WATER (FALL)

The kohl lined my eyes, deepening them, making them sharper—eyes that had seen love, loss, and the quiet acceptance of fate. A hint of blush dusted my cheeks, a colour that mimicked the warmth of emotions I wasn't sure I still felt. My lips, painted in a subtle shade of crimson, curved slightly, though I wasn't sure if it was a smile or just an illusion of one.

My hair, styled with precision, fell in cascading waves down my back, adorned with jasmine flowers that whispered stories of tradition and new beginnings. The weight of gold pressed against my skin—the necklace, the bangles, the earrings—each piece a reminder of the moment that was about to come.

The dupatta was finally draped over my head, its embroidered edges framing my face. I looked into the mirror again. A bride. A woman stepping into a new life. But somewhere, beneath the layers of silk and gold, beneath the carefully painted face, was a heart that still carried stories left untold.

Someone knocked at the door. 'It's time,' a voice called softly.

I took a deep breath, straightened my shoulders, and stood up. Today was not about the past. Today, I walked towards the future, taking my husband Vikram with me. I would heal him today.

The bangles on my wrists jingled softly as I turned to the door. My mother stood there, her face pale, her eyes brimming with tears that had already begun to fall.

'Mathura...' Her voice trembled, her hands clutching the edge of my dupatta. My breath hitched.

She took a step closer, struggling to find the words, but the silence between us already carried the weight of something terrible.

'It's Vikram... he—he had an accident.'

The room spun. The air thickened. For a moment, the sounds around me—the faint chatter of guests, the distant music, the rustling of fabric—faded into nothingness.

'What?' My voice barely escaped my lips.

'He's in the hospital... he's dead, Mathura,' she cried. I felt the blood drain from my face. My knees wobbled beneath the heavy lehenga, and I reached for the dressing table to steady myself. The mirror before me reflected not a bride but a woman on the edge of collapse.

Memories crashed over me all at once—his quiet smile, his unspoken pain, the love I had carried. I broke down and cried and cried.

He was the one who cared for me when I was alone.

He was the one who stood by me every time.

He was the one who kept me going, even when I wanted to give up.

He was the one who made me who I am today. He was the one in whom I see my family today.

He was the one who gave me the happiness I have today.

Just like stars that light up the night sky with their silent shine—maybe he was one of them, who would always shine bright for me. I wished I could cry while hugging him one

WATER (FALL)

last time. He was the only one I had, the only one who could lift me up again, the one who could make me happy again, the one who could be—my best friend again—my husband...

'I love you, Vikram. Thank you for everything.'

Acknowledgements

I would like to express my heartfelt appreciation to a few individuals:

Sir Neeraj Kumar Tibriwal, IFS and Sir Dinesh Kumar, IFS: thank you for your invaluable guidance, encouragement and support.

To Rajashekar sir, Keerthipal sir, Ganesh sir, Bhagya ma'am, Srikanth, Naresh, Ramesh—and all my colleagues— your support has meant so much to me. Without it, this book would never have been possible.

And to Sravanthi, Sai Pranay, Rahul, Rakshitha, Amrutha, Ashia, Avya, Teresa—your genuine encouragement and support are truly appreciated, which helped me stay motivated while writing this book.

About the Author

PALLE VASU (21) transitioned from working in the Forest Department to pursuing his passion for writing. Despite the rigorous demands of a 9 to 8 job, he rekindled his love for literature and dedicated himself to his craft. Follow him on Instagram: @palle_vasu

My life has been pretty messy. The character of Vikram was inspired by me, but life took its own course and led me to become an office subordinate (attendant) in the Forest Department. In the process,

About the Author

I lost everything that was once mine. Maybe this was my fate—and for a long time, I struggled with self-doubt.

But one thing I've come to realise is this: you are not always what you think you are. You have the power to change, starting today.

It takes months to write a book, but only days to read. If you enjoyed reading this book, please consider leaving a review on the platform where you purchased it. Your feedback means the world to me!

I have authored two more books: Forest Sentinel *and* Hurt Heal Growth. *Do read!*